DESTROY, SHE SAID

Works by Marguerite Duras
Published by Grove Press

The Malady of Death
India Song
Four Novels: The Square;
    10:30 on a Summer Night;
    The Afternoon of Mr. Andesmas;
    Moderato Cantabile
Hiroshima Mon Amour
Practicalities
Destroy, She Said

Marguerite Duras
DESTROY, SHE SAID
translated from the French by
Barbara Bray

DESTRUCTION AND LANGUAGE:
An Interview with
Marguerite Duras
translated from the French by
Helen Lane Cumberford

GROVE PRESS
New York

Published simultaneously in Canada
Printed in the United States of America

Library of Congress Cataloging-in-Publication Data

Duras, Marguerite.
  Destroy, she said.

  Translation of Detruire, dit-elle.
  "Destruction and language was originally published as La destruction la parole, in France, copyright © 1969 by Cahiers du cinema"—T.p. verso.
  I. Rivette, Jacques, 1928–   . Destruction la parole, English. 1986. II. Title. III. Title: Destruction and language.
PQ2607.U824D4713   1986   843'.912   86-45522
ISBN 978-0-8021-5154-4

Grove Press
an imprint of Grove/Atlantic, Inc.
154 West 14th Street
New York, NY 10011

Distributed by Publishers Group West
www.groveatlantic.com

14 15 16   10 9 8 7

For Dionys Mascolo

DESTROY, SHE SAID

*A*n overcast sky. The bay windows shut.

From where he is in the dining room he can't see outside.

But she can. She is looking out. Her table touches the windowsill.

The light makes her screw up her eyes. They move to and fro. Some of the other guests are watching the tennis matches too. But he can't see.

He hasn't asked to be moved to another table, though.

She doesn't know she is being watched.

It rained this morning about five.

Today the air the balls thud through is close and heavy. She is wearing a summer dress.

The book is in front of her. Begun since he arrived? or before?

Beside the book are two bottles of white pills. She takes some at every meal. Sometimes she opens the book. Then shuts it again almost at once. And looks at the tennis matches.

On other tables are other bottles and other books.

Her hair is black, greyish black, smooth, not in good condition, dry. You can't tell what color her eyes are. Even when she turns back toward the room they're still blinded by the glaring light near the window. Round the eyes, when she smiles, the flesh is already delicately lined. She is very pale.

None of the people in the hotel play tennis. The players are local boys and girls. No one minds.

"It's pleasant to have the youngsters about. And they're very considerate."

No one but he has noticed her.

"You get used to the noise."

When he arrived six days ago she was already there, the book and the pills in front of her. She was muffled up in a long jacket and black slacks. It was cool.

He noticed how well-dressed she was, her figure, then the way she moved, the way she slept on the grounds every day, her hands.

Someone telephones.

The first time she was in the grounds. He didn't listen to the name. The second time he couldn't catch it.

So someone phones after her afternoon nap. By arrangement, no doubt.

Sunshine. The seventh day.

There she is again, by the tennis courts, on a white chaise-longue. There are other white chaises-longues, mostly empty, empty and lying stranded face to face, or in circles, or alone.

After her nap he loses sight of her.

He watches her from the balcony as she sleeps. She is tall, and looks as if she were dead, just slightly bent at the hips. She is slim; thin.

The courts are deserted at this hour. Tennis is not

4

allowed during nap time. It starts again about four and
goes on till dusk.

The seventh day. But the torpor of the siesta is shattered by a man's voice, sharp, almost brutal.

No one answers. He wasn't talking to anyone.

No one wakes.

She's the only one so near the tennis courts. The
others are farther away, either in the shade under the
hedges or on the grass in the sun.

The voice that just spoke goes on echoing through
the hotel grounds.

Day. The eighth. Sunshine. It's hot now.

Though she is usually so punctual, she wasn't there
when he went into the dining room at lunchtime. She
came in after they had started serving, smiling, calm,
less pale. He'd known she must still be there because
of the book and the pills, her place set as usual, and
because there had been no stir in the hotel corridors
during the morning. No arrivals, no departures. So he
knew, quite logically, that she hadn't left.

When she comes in she walks past his table.

She sits in profile facing the windows. This makes it
easier for him to keep watch on her.

She is beautiful. But it is invisible.

Does she know?

"No. No."

The voice dies away over by the gate into the forest.

No one answers. It is the same voice—sharp, almost
brutal.

5

Not a cloud in the sky today. The heat is increasing, becoming settled, permeating the forest, the grounds of the hotel.

"Almost oppressive, don't you think?"

Blue blinds have been let down over the windows. Her table is in the blue light coming through them. It makes her hair black, her eyes blue.

Today the balls seem to thud right through your head and your heart.

Dusk in the hotel. She sits on in the neon light of the dining room, drained of color, older.

With a sudden nervous gesture she pours some water into her glass, opens the bottles, takes out some pills and swallows them.

It's the first time she's taken twice the prescribed dose.

It's still light outside. Nearly everyone has gone. The bay windows are open. A breeze comes in through the stiff net curtains.

She grows calmer.

He has picked up the book, his book, and opens it. He doesn't read.

Voices can be heard from the grounds.

She goes out.

She has gone out.

He shuts the book.

Nine o'clock, dusk, dusk in the hotel and over the forest.

"Do you mind?"

He looks up and recognizes him. He has been here in the hotel all the time, since the first day. He's always seen him there, yes, either in the grounds, or the dining room, or in the corridors, yes, always, or in the road that runs by the hotel, round the tennis courts, at night, in the daytime, wandering round and round, round and round, alone. His age doesn't strike one. His eyes do.

He sits down, takes out a cigarette, offers him one.

"I'm not disturbing you?"

"Not at all."

"I'm here alone too, you see."

"Yes."

She stands up. Walks past.

He is silent.

"We're always the last, every evening. Look, they've all gone." His voice is sharp, almost brutal. "Are you a writer?"

"No. Why are you speaking to me today?"

"I sleep badly. I dread going to my room. I toss and turn, my thoughts wear me out."

They are silent.

"You haven't answered my question. Why today?"

He looks at him at last.

"You were expecting it?"

"I suppose I was."

He gets up, makes a gesture of invitation.

"Shall we go over by the windows?"

"There's no point in it."

"All right."

He hasn't heard her go up the stairs. She must have gone out in the garden to wait for it to be completely dark. But he can't be sure.

"All the people here are tired, had you noticed? No children or dogs or papers or television."

"Is that why you're here?"

"No. It's the same here to me as it would be anywhere else. I come back every year. I'm not an invalid any more than you are. No. This place has memories for me. They wouldn't interest you. I met a woman here."

"And she hasn't come back?"

"She must have died."

He says everything in the same monotonous voice.

"There could be other explanations," he adds. "But that's what I think."

"But you come back in the hope of finding her?"

"Oh no, I don't think so. You mustn't think it was a . . . oh no. But she kept me interested a whole summer. That was all."

"Why?"

He pauses before answering. He rarely looks anyone in the eye.

"I couldn't say. It was a question of me—me and her together. Do you see? Shall we go over by the windows?"

They get up and cross the empty dining room. They stand by the windows, facing the grounds. Yes, that's where she was. She is walking round the tennis courts, dressed in black today. She's smoking. All the guests are outside. He doesn't look out into the grounds.

"My name's Stein," he says. "I'm a Jew."

There she goes, past the porch. Now she's gone.

"Did you hear what I said my name was?"

"Yes—Stein. It must be quite cool now. I thought they were all in bed. But they're all outside."

"Today the balls seemed to thud right through your head and your heart, didn't they?"

"Yes."

Silence.

"My wife's coming to get me in a few days. We're taking a vacation."

His smooth face becomes even more inscrutable. Is he brooding?

"I never imagined that."

"What did you think?"

"Nothing. I didn't think anything," Stein says.

Four people have taken it into their heads to play croquet at this hour. You can hear them laughing.

"What energy!" he says.

"Don't change the subject."

"My wife is very young. Young enough to be my daughter."

"What's her name?"

"Alissa."

"I thought you had no attachments outside the hotel." He smiles. "No one ever phones you. You don't get any letters. And now here all of a sudden Alissa is going to put in an appearance."

She halts by a path—the path that leads to the forest—hesitates, then walks toward the porch of the hotel.

"In three days. At the moment Alissa's staying with

9

her family. We've been married two years. She goes to see her family every year. She's been there about ten days. I can scarcely remember what she looks like."

She has come indoors again. Those are her footsteps. She's going along the corridor.

"I've lived with various women," Stein says. "You and I are about the same age, so I've had plenty of time for women. But I've never married any of them. I may have gone through the pretenses, but never without an inner howl of refusal. Never."

Now she's on the stairs.

"And you? Are you a writer?"

"I'm in the process of becoming one," says Stein. "Do you see?"

"Yes. I suppose it's always been like that?"

"Yes. How did you guess?"

No longer any sound of any kind. She must have gone into her room.

"How?" Stein asks again.

"By the way you keep asking questions. Questions that get you nowhere."

They look at each other and smile.

Stein points out at the grounds and beyond.

"Outside the grounds," he says, "six miles or so from the hotel, there's a very well-known view. You can see all the hills that underlie this region."

"Is that where everyone is when the hotel's empty in the afternoon?"

"Yes. They always come back by dusk, have you noticed?"

Silence.

"Anything else here besides the view?"

"I've never heard of anything else worth seeing. No . . . nothing apart from that. Only the forest. It's there all round us."

Darkness swallows up the tops of the trees. No color left anywhere.

"I only know the grounds," Max Thor says. "I haven't been outside."

Silence.

"At the end of the main path," says Max Thor, "there's a gate."

"Oh, you've noticed it?"

"Yes."

"They don't go into the forest."

"Oh, you knew that too?" Stein says.

"No. I didn't know."

Silence.

Then Stein goes as he came—without hesitation, without warning. He walks out of the dining room with his long indefatigable stride. Once out in the grounds he walks more slowly. He walks about among the others. He scrutinizes them without any restraint. He never speaks to them.

Sunshine and heat in the grounds.

She has changed her position on the chaise-longue. She has turned over and gone to sleep again, her legs stretched out and parted, her arm bent up over her face. Until today he had avoided going past her. Today, coming back from the far side of the grounds, he does just that, he walks past her. His footsteps on the gravel pierce the stillness of the sleeping body, make it start.

The arm lifts slightly, and two eyes gaze at him from under it, unseeing. He walks by. The body goes still again. The eyes close.

Stein was coming down the steps of the hotel absentmindedly. They pass each other.

"I tremble all the time," says Stein, in a sort of trembling uncertainty.

Dark. Dark, except for gleams of light on the other side of the grounds.

Stein is there beside him nearly every evening now. He comes after dinner. She is still at table. To her right, one last lingering couple. She is waiting. What for?

A sudden lurid glow of the last light.

Stein and he have left the table. They are sitting in a couple of armchairs facing her. A lamp is on. Two mirrors reflect the setting sun.

"Madame Elisabeth Alione is wanted on the telephone."

A clear, high, airport voice. Stein doesn't move.

She gets up and goes across the dining room. She walks easily. Smiles mechanically as she goes past the armchairs. Disappears into the hall.

The last couple leave. In the silence, no sound from the telephone booth, beyond the office in the other wing of the hotel.

Stein gets up and goes over to the bay windows.

Someone switches the dining room lights off, thinking everyone's gone.

"She won't come back again this evening," says Stein.

"Did you know the name?"

"I must have. I must have known and forgotten. It wasn't a surprise to me."

He peers out into the grounds.

"They're all outside," he says. "Except her. And us. She doesn't like the evening."

"You're wrong. She always goes out in the garden after dinner."

"Not for long. And she always hurries in."

He walks back calmly and sits down again beside him. He looks at him for a long while without expression.

"Last night," says Stein, "when I was outside, I saw you sitting at your desk writing. Slowly. With difficulty. Your hand hovered over the page a long time. Then started writing again. And then suddenly it gave up. You stood up and came out on the balcony."

"I sleep badly. Like you."

"We both sleep badly."

"Yes. I listen. To the dogs. To the walls creaking. Till my head spins round. Then I write something."

"That's it. What? A letter?"

"Perhaps. But who to? Who to? In the dead of night, in the empty hotel, who to write to, that's the question, isn't it?"

"Well," says Stein, "the exciting things that happen to us at night, you and me. I walk about the grounds. Sometimes I hear my own voice."

"I've seen you sometimes. Heard you too, just before daybreak."

"That's right. That's me. The dogs in the distance, and my voice."

They look at each other in silence.

"Have you got it with you?" says Stein.

He takes the white envelope out of his pocket and gives it to Stein. Stein opens it, unfolds the letter, is silent a moment, then reads.

" 'Madame,' " he reads, " 'Madame, I have been watching you for ten days. There's something about you that fascinates me, puts me in a turmoil, and I can't, I simply can't, make out what it is.' "

Stein stops, then goes on.

" 'Madame, I would like to get to know you. I wouldn't expect anything out of it for myself.' "

Stein puts the letter back in the envelope and the envelope down on the table.

"How quiet it is," Stein says. "Who'd believe our nights are such an ordeal?"

Stein leans back in his chair. They are both in the same position.

"You don't know anything?" Stein asks.

"Nothing. Only the face. And the way she sleeps."

Stein switches on the lamp between the two chairs and looks at him.

Silence.

"She doesn't get any letters either," Stein goes on. "But someone telephones. Usually after her siesta. She wears a wedding ring. But no one has come to see her yet."

Silence.

Stein gets up slowly and goes out.

While Stein is gone the other man gets up, goes over to Elisabeth Alione's table, and puts his hand out toward the book, which is shut. But he draws back and doesn't turn it over.

Stein comes back with the hotel register. They go and sit down again under the lamp.

"They're never in the office at this hour," he says. "It was easy."

He leafs through the register, stops.

"Here she is," Stein says.

"Alione," Stein says very clearly. He goes on reading slowly, and more quietly. "Alione. Maiden name: Villeneuve. Born Grenoble, March 10, 1931. Occupation: none. Nationality: French. Address: 5 avenue Magenta, Grenoble. Date of arrival: July 2."

Stein riffles through the pages and stops again.

"And here you are," says Stein. "Right next to her. 'Thor. Max Thor, born Paris, June 20, 1929. Occupation: university professor. Nationality: French. Address: 4 rue Camille-Dubois, Paris. Arrived July 4."

He shuts the register, goes out, comes back at once and sits down again beside Max Thor.

"So we know something," he says. "We're gradually getting somewhere. We know about Grenoble. And the words: Villeneuve, Elisabeth—Villeneuve at eighteen!"

Stein seems to be listening. Someone is walking about overhead.

"They've gone up to bed," he says. "We could take a walk outside now, if you like? There are still lights in the bedroom windows."

Max Thor doesn't move.

"Alissa," says Max Thor. "Alissa. I'm impatient for her to get here."

"Come," says Stein gently.

He gets up. They start to go. Before they reach the door Stein points to the letter on the table.

"Are we going to leave it on the table?"

"No one ever comes by here," says Max Thor. "And there's no name on it."

"Are you leaving it there for Alissa?"

"Oh . . . yes, perhaps for Alissa," Max Thor says.

He points to Elisabeth Alione's table.

"She's been reading the same novel for a week," he says. "The same shape, the same cover. She must keep starting it and forgetting what she's read and starting it all over again. Did you know?"

"Yes."

"What kind of a book is it?"

Stein ponders.

"Would you like me to see? I can allow myself to do things you wouldn't do."

"As you like."

Stein goes over to Elisabeth Alione's table, opens the book at the title-page and comes back.

"It's nothing," Stein says. "A bookrack novel. Nothing."

"That's what I thought," Max Thor says.

Dazzling light. It has rained during the morning. Sunday.

"My brothers were there with their wives and children," says Alissa. "The house was full."

Elisabeth Alione opens the book. Max Thor listens to Alissa.

16

"I must say it was very gay, especially in the evenings. Mother stays very young."

Elisabeth Alione shuts the book. Her table is set for three. She looks toward the dining room door. She's in black. The bay windows are closed.

"You haven't changed your mind? We're still going there for Christmas?"

"I'd like to go for a few days, yes."

"I wonder why you get so bored there," says Alissa, smiling. "They're no more boring than most people ... at least, I don't think so."

"I feel rather awkward there. I'm not much younger than your mother."

"I've sometimes thought I'm too young."

Max Thor looks surprised.

"I've never thought about it. Except to realize I'll probably end up alone. But I accepted the idea of that desertion from the beginning."

"So did I."

They laugh.

And while Stein crosses the dining room, Elisabeth Alione gets up and smiles too, looking toward the door. A man and a little girl have just come in. Alissa looks at the man.

"Enter provincial heart-throb," Alissa says.

"Anita," Elisabeth Alione says.

The voice is distant, gentle, what you'd have expected. They've kissed each other and sat down.

"What sort of people are there here?"

"Invalids," he smiles wryly. "I suddenly noticed it last Sunday. Their families come in the morning and go away again in the evening. There aren't any children."

Alissa turns round and looks.

"Yes, I see ... But you don't want to leave right away?"

"Did I say that?"

"Yes, in the room, when I arrived."

"Oh, we could stay on just a few days. Or we could go tomorrow as planned."

Silence.

"Perhaps you don't really feel like going away this year," Alissa says after a pause. She smiles. "You've traveled such a lot already ..."

"It's not that."

They look at each other.

"I feel comfortable here, almost happy."

Anita must be about fourteen.

Elisabeth Alione's husband may be younger than she is.

"Almost happy?"

"I mean at ease."

Stein goes by again, with a brief nod to Max Thor. Alissa looks at Stein intently.

"That's a fellow called Stein. We talk sometimes."

The first couples begin to leave the dining room. Alissa doesn't see them.

"Stein," says Max Thor. "He's a Jew, too."

"Stein."

"Yes."

Alissa looks over towards the bay windows.

"It is pleasant here. Especially with the grounds."

She listens.

"Where are the tennis courts?"

18

"Just outside, right next to the hotel."

Alissa freezes.

"And then there's the forest," she says.

Now, suddenly, she looks only at the forest.

"Yes."

"Is it dangerous?" she asks.

"Yes. How did you know?"

"I'm looking at it," she says. "I can see it."

She ponders, still looking beyond the hotel grounds to the forest.

"Why is it dangerous?" she asks.

"I don't know, any more than you do. Why?"

"Because they're afraid of it," Alissa says.

She leans back in her chair and looks at him fixedly.

"I don't feel hungry any more."

Her voice has suddenly changed, grown faint.

"I'm so happy you're here," he says.

She looks around. Then brings her eyes back, slowly.

"Destroy," she says.

He smiles at her.

"Yes. Let's go upstairs before we go outside."

"Yes."

Elisabeth Alione is crying silently. It's not a scene. The man only banged on the table quite lightly; only he could see she's crying, and he's not looking.

"I haven't got to know anyone. Except Stein."

"Did you say something just now about being 'happy'?"

"No . . . I don't think so."

"Happy in this hotel. Happy. How strange."

"I'm rather surprised myself."

Elisabeth Alione is crying because she wants to go home. He doesn't want her to. The daughter has got up and gone out into the garden.

"Why's that woman crying?" Alissa asks softly. "There, just behind me."

"How did you know?" Max Thor cries.

No one turns round.

Alissa tries to think. Then indicates she doesn't know how she knew. Max Thor is calm again.

"That sort of thing often happens when there are visitors," he says.

She looks at him.

"You're tired."

He smiles.

"I'm not sleeping very well."

She shows no surprise. Her voice grows fainter still.

"Sometimes the silence stops one sleeping—the forest, or the silence?"

"Perhaps, yes."

"Or being in a hotel room?"

"It could be that."

Alissa's voice is now almost inaudible. Her eyes are huge, deep blue.

"It might be an idea to stay on a few days," she says.

She gets up. She totters slightly. Elisabeth and her husband are the only ones left in the dining room. Stein has come back.

"I'm going outside," Alissa murmurs.

Max Thor stands up. He meets Stein in the hall. He is radiant with happiness.

20

"You didn't tell me Alissa was insane," says Stein.
"I didn't know," says Max Thor.

Outside. Day. Sunday.

Elisabeth Alione and her family approach Alissa and Max Thor and walk past them toward the porch. A man's voice:

"The doctor was very firm about it. You must get plenty of sleep."

Elisabeth has her arm round Anita's waist. She smiles. A child's voice:

"We'll come again one last time."

Is Alissa watching? Yes.

They are sitting in the shadow of a tree. Elisabeth walks slowly back in their direction. Alissa shuts her eyes. Elisabeth lies down on her chaise-longue. She too shuts her eyes. Her smile of farewell gradually fades, leaving her face completely expressionless.

"Is she an invalid too?" asks Alissa.

Her voice is low and flat.

"I expect so. She sleeps every afternoon."

"All you can hear now is the birds," Alissa wails.

She shuts her eyes.

Silence. Wind.

Elisabeth Alione opens her eyes, pulls a white rug up over her.

Silence.

"Don't worry," Max Thor says.

"Something's happened, hasn't it?"

"I don't know."

Here's Stein, coming out of the hotel.

"Something I can understand?"

"Yes."

Stein doesn't stop beside them, but he looks at them as he goes by. They both lie there with their eyes shut. Both are pale. Stein walks with long hesitant strides toward the far side of the grounds.

"There's something in this hotel that troubles and intrigues me. I can't quite make out what it is. I don't really try. Others might say it had to do with old desires, the dreams one has as a child ..."

Alissa doesn't move.

"Write it down, perhaps," says Max Thor. "Because here it's as if I understood how one might ..." He smiles, his eyes still shut. "Every night since I've been here I've been on the point of beginning ... I don't write, I never shall ... and every night what I'd write if I did write changes."

"So it's at night it happens."

"Yes."

Silence. His eyes are closed.

"You look happy," she says.

Silence.

"I was talking to you."

"Yes. I don't understand. I don't understand yet," she says.

He doesn't answer.

Stein is coming back.

Max Thor doesn't see him.

Stein is walking toward them.

"Here comes Stein," says Alissa.

"Let him," cries Max Thor. He calls out: "Here we are, Stein—over here."

"He's coming."

Stein is here.

"I came too soon," Alissa cries.

Stein doesn't answer. He looks round the garden, at the people sleeping. No one has moved since he went by before. Stein stands by Alissa gazing down at her.

"I don't understand, I don't understand yet," she cries to him.

He still stands looking down at her.

"Alissa," he says, "he was waiting for you, he was counting the days."

"That's what I mean," Alissa cries.

Stein doesn't answer. Since he came up to them Max Thor seems to have sunk into deep repose.

"Perhaps we love each other too much?" asks Alissa. "Perhaps the love between us is too great, between him and me, too strong, much, much too strong?"

She goes on, her voice still raised. "Perhaps between him and me, just between him and me, there's too much love?"

Stein doesn't answer.

She stops. Looks at Stein.

"I'll never cry out like that again," Alissa says.

She smiles at him. Her eyes are huge and deep blue.

"Stein," she says softly.

"Yes."

"Stein, he was there without me, at night, in his room. Everything had begun to exist again without me, even the night."

"No," says Max Thor, "the night could never exist without you now."

"But I wasn't there," Alissa cries faintly, "either in the room or outside."

Silence. Sudden silence.

"You *were* in the grounds," says Stein. "You were in the grounds already."

She points to Max, who still has his eyes shut.

"Perhaps he doesn't know," she says to Stein. "Doesn't know what has happened to him?"

"He doesn't," says Stein.

"Meeting you wasn't indispensable any more," says Max Thor to Alissa.

He opens his eyes and looks at them. They don't look at him.

"That's what I know," he says.

"There's no point in suffering, Alissa," says Stein. "No point."

Stein sits down on the path, looks at Alissa's body, forgets. A little way away, Elisabeth Alione has turned over towards the porch of the hotel and fallen asleep again.

Silence. Silence about Alissa.

"Stein," asks Alissa, "do you sleep out here in the grounds?"

"Yes. All over the place."

Max Thor puts out his hand and takes the icy hand of Alissa, his wife, shattered into a blue stare.

"Don't suffer any more, Alissa," Stein says.

Stein comes nearer, rests his head on Alissa's bare knees. He strokes, then kisses them.

24

"I want you so much," Max Thor says.

"He wants you so much," Stein says. "He loves you so much."

Dusk. Grey.

It's still light enough for tennis. The balls thud through the grey dusk.

It's still light near the bay windows, too, though farther inside the dining room the lamps are on.

The windows are open. The hot spell is lasting. Elisabeth Alione gets up and goes over to the windows. She looks first at the tennis courts, then at the grounds.

"If we hadn't yet met," says Alissa to Max Thor, "we wouldn't have said a word. I'd be sitting at this table. You'd be sitting at another—alone, like me." She stops. "Stein wouldn't be there, would he? Not yet?"

"Not yet. Stein comes later."

Alissa looks fixedly at the part of the dining room that's already dark. She points toward it.

"There," she says. "You'd be there. You there. I here. We'd be separated. Separated by the tables, the bedroom walls." She opens her clenched fists and says in a faint cry: "Still separated."

Silence.

"There'd be our first words," Max Thor says.

"No," Alissa cries.

"Our first glances," Max Thor says.

"Perhaps. No, no."

Silence. Her hands are back on the table.

"I'm trying to understand," she says.

Silence. Elisabeth Alione is leaning out of one of the windows, her body outlined against the square of grey air beneath the open window.

"What would it be like?" asks Max Thor.

She tries to think.

"A grey dusk," she says at last. She points to it. "I'd be watching the tennis matches and you'd come up to me. I wouldn't hear anything. And suddenly you'd be there. You'd watch too."

She hasn't made any actual reference to Elisabeth Alione, who is watching now.

Silence fills the hotel. Has the tennis playing stopped?

"You're trying to understand, too," she says.

"Yes. Perhaps there'd be a letter?"

"Yes, perhaps."

"I'd have been watching you for ten days," says Max Thor.

"Yes. Just left lying about, without any address. I'd find it."

No, there goes the tennis again. The balls ping in a liquid dusk, a grey lake. Elisabeth Alione pulls up a chair and quietly sits down. The game is a lively one.

"But it has happened, hasn't it?"

He hesitates.

"Perhaps," he says.

"Yes. Perhaps it's not certain."

She smiles, leaning toward him.

"Maybe we ought to separate every summer," she says. "Forget one another, if that were possible?"

"It's possible." He calls out to her: "Alissa, Alissa."

She is deaf. She suddenly speaks, slowly, clearly.

26

"It's only when you're there that I can forget you," she says. "How's the book getting on? Are you thinking about it?"

"No, I'm talking to you."

She is silent.

"Who's the book about?"

"Max Thor."

"What does he do?"

"Nothing. Someone is watching."

She turns toward Elisabeth Alione, who is sitting up straight, in profile, looking at the tennis matches.

"A woman, for example?" asks Alissa.

"Yes. Perhaps. You, if I don't know you, or that woman watching."

"Watching what?"

"The games of tennis, I think."

It's as if Alissa didn't register the allusion to Elisabeth Alione.

"People are always looking at the tennis courts. Even when they're empty, even when it's raining. They do it mechanically."

"In the book I haven't written there was only you," Alissa says.

"How strongly," says Max Thor, smiling, "how strongly sometimes one feels one mustn't write that book. I shall never write any books."

"Can one really say a thing like that?"

"Yes, and mean it."

"Stein will write," says Alissa. "So we don't need to."

"Yes."

Elisabeth Alione walks with her tranquil gait out of the light near the bay windows. She brushes by the empty tables, theirs included. She keeps her eyes lowered. Max Thor glances almost imperceptibly toward Alissa, who apparently watches Elisabeth without particular attention.

She has gone. They are silent.

"So it would be about the tennis courts?" asks Alissa.

"Yes. The tennis courts being looked at."

"By a woman?"

"Yes. Preoccupied."

"By what?"

"The void."

"Would it be about the tennis courts empty at night, too?" Alissa goes on.

"Yes."

"They look like cages," she says dreamily. "Would you make things up in your book?"

"No. I'd describe."

"Stein?"

"No. Stein looks *for* me. I'd describe what he looks at."

Alissa gets up, goes over to the bay windows, comes back. Max Thor looks at her fragile form.

"I wanted to see what she was looking at," says Alissa.

"You're so young," says Max Thor, "that when you walk . . ."

She doesn't answer.

"What do you do all day? All night?"

"Nothing."

"You don't read?"

"No. I pretend to."

"How far along are you with the book?"

"Stuck in endless preliminaries."

He has got up. They look at each other. Her eyes are shining.

"It's a good subject," says Alissa. "The best."

"Sometimes I talk to Stein. This state can't last more than a few days."

She is in his arms. But she pushes him away.

"Go out in the grounds," she tells him. "Disappear in the grounds. Let it eat you up."

As they kiss the lights go out and the two chairs on the other side of the room are illuminated, picked out.

"I'll come," says Alissa. "I'll come out in the grounds with you."

Max Thor goes out. Alissa runs to the armchair and throws herself into it, her head in her hands.

Complete darkness.

The lights are on in the grounds. In the dining room, Alissa is still outlined against the armchair. Stein appears. He goes over to Alissa, sits down near her without saying anything, calmly. On the table is a white envelope.

"Alissa," he says at last. "It's Stein."

"Stein."

"Yes. I'm here."

She doesn't move. Stein slides down onto the floor and rests his head on her knees.

"I don't know you, Alissa," Stein says.

"Perhaps he's stopped loving me in a certain way?"

"It was here he realized he couldn't imagine his life any more without you." He uses the familiar "tu." From now on they both do.

They are silent. He places his hands on her body.

"You're part of me, Alissa. Your fragile body is part of mine. And I don't know you."

A clear high airport voice calls through the grounds: "Elisabeth Alione is wanted on the telephone."

"What a lovely name that woman has," says Alissa. "The one who was watching the tennis courts before you came. Elisabeth Alione. That's an Italian name."

"She was here when he came."

"Always alone?"

"Nearly always. Her husband comes sometimes."

"Yesterday—was that idiot at her table him?"

"Yes."

"She was crying. Apart from that, she always looks half asleep. She takes sedatives. I've seen her. She must take more than she should."

"So they say."

"Yes. She's not striking at first sight, and then suddenly she becomes so . . . It's strange . . . She walks well. And she sleeps lightly, almost like a child . . ."

She sits up and takes Stein's head in her hands.

"You can't talk to me, can you?"

"No."

"This is the first time it's been impossible for him and me to talk to one another. The first time he's hidden anything from me . . ."

"Yes."

"He doesn't really know what it is, does he?"

"He only knows everything would go if you went."

She picks the letter up slowly and opens the envelope.

"Stein, look at it with me."

Side by side, almost indistinguishable from one another, they read:

" 'Alissa knows,' " Stein reads. " 'But what does she know?' "

Quite calmly Alissa puts the letter back in the envelope and tears it up.

"I wrote it for you," says Stein, "before I knew you'd guessed."

They go over, arms entwined, to the bay windows.

"Has she come back from the telephone?" asks Alissa.

"Yes."

"He isn't with her? Isn't he talking to someone? Look, Stein. Look for me."

"No, no one. He never talks to anyone. You can hardly get a word out of him. He only speaks when he's spoken to. A whole part of him is dumb. He's sitting waiting."

"We make love," Alissa says. "Every night we make love."

"I know," says Stein. "You leave the window open and I see you."

"He leaves it open for you. To see us."

"Yes."

Alissa has put her childish lips on Stein's hard mouth. He speaks like that.

"Do you see us?" Alissa says.

"Yes. You don't say anything. Every night I wait. Silence clamps you to the bed. The light stays on and on. One morning they'll find you both melted into a shapeless lump like tar, and no one will understand. Except me."

Day in the garden. Sun.

Alissa Thor and Elisabeth Alione are lying about thirty feet apart. Alissa is watching Elisabeth Alione through half-shut eyes.

Elisabeth Alione is asleep, her unprotected face bent slightly on one shoulder. Her body is dappled with patches of sunlight filtering through the leaves. The sun shines steadily. The air is perfectly still. Alissa, in a series of dazzling insights, discovers the body under the dress, the long lean-thighed runner's legs, the extraordinary flexibility of the sleeping hands hanging from the wrists, the waist, the dry mass of hair, the position of the eyes.

From behind the dining room window Max Thor looks out on the grounds. Alissa doesn't see him. She is turned toward Elisabeth Alione. All Max Thor can see of Alissa is her hair, her legs on the chaise-longue, and that she's pretending to be asleep.

Max Thor remains for a moment looking out at the grounds. When he turns around Stein is there.

"They've all gone for a
walk," Stein says. "We're
alone."
Silence.
The windows are open
onto the grounds.
"How quiet," Stein says.
"You can hear them breath-
ing."
Silence.
"Alissa knows," Max Thor
says. "But what does she
know?"
Stein doesn't answer.

Alissa has stood up. She is walking barefoot along
the path. She goes past Elisabeth Alione. She seems to
hesitate. Yes. She comes back to where Elisabeth Alione is and stands there a moment opposite her. Then
she goes over to her own chaise-longue and moves it a
few yards, nearer to Elisabeth Alione.

Max Thor's face, seem-
ingly suspended at the window, suddenly turns away.
Stein doesn't move.

Elisabeth Alione slowly wakes. It was the scraping of
the other chaise-longue on the gravel that awoke her.
They smile at each other.

33

Max Thor has drawn back
and is not looking again
yet. He stands there rigid,
his eyes half-shut.

"You were right in the sun," Alissa says.

"I can sleep right in the sun."

"I can't."

"It's a habit. I can go to sleep just as easily on the beach."

"She's spoken," says Stein.
Max Thor comes over
and looks.

"Her voice is the same as
when she spoke to Anita,"
he says.

"Just as easily?" Alissa asks.

"It's cold where I come from," says Elisabeth Alione. "So I can never get enough sun."

Alissa's blue eyes look intriguing in the shadows.

"You've just arrived."

"No, I've been here three days."

"Really?"

"We're quite close to one another in the dining room."

"I don't see very well," Elisabeth Alione says. Then, smiling: "In fact I can't see a thing. I usually wear glasses."

"But not here?"

34

She makes a little grimace.
"No. I'm here convalescing. It rests my eyes."

> "Where did you meet Alissa?" Stein asks.
> "Asleep," says Max Thor, "in one of my lectures."
> "I see," Stein says.
> "That's what most of my students do. I've forgotten everything I know."
> "I see. Fine."

"Convalescing?" Alissa asks.
Elisabeth Alione screws up her eyes to look at the woman listening so intently.
"I'm here because of a confinement that went wrong. The baby was born dead. It was a little girl."
She sits up straight, runs her hands through her hair, smiles painfully at Alissa.
"I take medicine to make me sleep. I sleep all the time."
Alissa has sat up too.
"It must have been a great shock?"
"Yes. I couldn't sleep any more."
She speaks more slowly:
"And it had been a difficult pregnancy."

> "Here comes the lie," Max Thor says.
> "It's still a long way off."

35

"Yes, she doesn't know
about it yet."

"A difficult pregnancy?" asks Alissa.
"Yes. Very."
They are silent.
"And you still think about it a lot?"
The question has made her start. Her cheeks are less
pale than they were.
"I don't know . . ." She corrects herself. "I mean,
I'm not supposed to, you see . . . And then I sleep a
lot . . . I could have gone to stay with my parents in
the South. But the doctor said I ought to be quite
alone."

"Total destruction will
come first through Alissa,"
Stein says. "Don't you
agree?"
"Yes. And do you agree
she isn't altogether safe?"
"Yes," Stein says. "Alissa
isn't altogether safe."

"Quite alone?" Alissa asks.
"Yes."
"For how long?"
"Three weeks. I came on July 2."
A wave of deep silence passes over the hotel and
grounds. A tremor has gone through Elisabeth Alione.

"Was there someone there?"—she points—"on the other side of the grounds?"

Alissa looks round.

"It could only be Stein, if it's anyone," Alissa says.

Silence.

"Perhaps you needed to get a grip on yourself, on your own, without anyone to help you," Alissa says.

"Perhaps. I didn't ask any questions."

She looks as if she were waiting. She stares at the grounds intently.

"Soon they'll all be coming back from their walk," she says.

> "She looks at the void," Stein says.
>
> "That's the only thing she looks at. But she does it well."
>
> "That's right," Max Thor says. "It's the way she does it that..."

"Yes, they'll soon be back," Alissa says.

"Oh ... I wish I could wake up," Elisabeth says.

She stands up, as if she suddenly didn't feel well. Alissa doesn't move.

"Were you told to walk for a bit every day?"

"Yes. Half an hour. There's no reason why not."

Elisabeth moves her chaise-longue nearer to Alissa and sits down again. They are quite close. Elisabeth Alione's eyes are very light.

37

She has to make a visible effort to look at Alissa. And now she suddenly sees Alissa's face for the first time.

"We could go for a walk together if you like . . ." she says.

"In a moment," Alissa says.

> "Did you want Alissa as soon as you saw her?" Stein asks.
>
> "No," Max Thor says. "I didn't want anyone. And you?"
>
> "As soon as she walked through the door," says Stein.

"In a moment," Alissa says. "It's early yet."

"The second doctor I saw," says Elisabeth Alione, "said the opposite. He wanted me to go somewhere cheerful with lots of people. But my husband thought the first doctor was more sensible."

"What do you think?"

"Oh . . . I did as they wanted . . . It's all the same to me. The forest's supposed to be restful."

Here come the tennis players. They don't see the two women. Alissa and Elisabeth Alione look at the tennis courts.

Alissa has smiled, but Elisabeth hasn't noticed.

"You don't play tennis?"

"I don't know how . . . And then I was . . . the confinement was . . . I'm not supposed to exert myself."

"Torn," says Max Thor.
"Bloody."
"Yes."

"Do you go into the forest?"

"Oh no. Not on my own. Have you seen it?"

"Not yet. I've only just arrived. I've only been here three days."

"Of course . . . Perhaps you're ill too?"

"No." Alissa laughs. "We're here by mistake. We thought it was just an ordinary hotel. I can't remember who recommended it . . . Someone at the university, I expect. They specially mentioned the forest."

"Oh."

Elisabeth Alione suddenly feels hot. She throws back her head in search of air.

"How muggy it is," she says. "What *is* the time?"

Alissa gestures that she doesn't know.

They are silent.

"Two years ago, the night she came to my place, Alissa was eighteen," Max Thor says.

"In the bedroom," says Stein slowly, "in the bedroom Alissa isn't any age."

"Did you want the child very much?" asks Alissa.

She hesitates.

"I think so . . . the question didn't arise."

"Alissa only believes in
the Rosenfeld theory," Stein
says. "Did you know?"

"Yes. You did too, I sup
pose?"

"I've just found out."

"Well..." says Elisabeth Alione, "it was my husband really ... he wanted another child. I was terribly
afraid he'd be disappointed. I used to get terribly
frightened ... that he wouldn't love me any more because the baby was ... But I mustn't talk about it. The
doctor said I wasn't to."

"And you listen to him?"

"Yes. Why?"

Her eyes question her. Alissa waits.

"You needn't listen to anyone," Alissa says gently.
"You can do as you like."

Elisabeth Alione smiles.

"I don't want to."

"Would you like to come into the forest?"

Suddenly, a glint of fear in Elisabeth Alione's eyes.

"Are we going to let her
go into the forest with
Alissa?" Max Thor asks.

"No," Stein says. "No."

"I'm here," Alissa says. "Don't be afraid."

"There's no point." She gives a hostile look at the
forest. "No, no point."

"Would you be afraid, with me?"

"No . . . but what's the point?"

Alissa gives up.

"You're afraid of me," she says softly.

Elisabeth Alione gives an embarrassed smile.

"Oh no, it's not that . . . It's just that . . ."

"What?"

"It terrifies me."

"You can't see it," Alissa says, smiling.

"Oh . . . that's what people think," she says.

"No," Alissa says softly. "You were afraid of me. Only a little. But you were afraid nonetheless."

Elisabeth looks at Alissa.

"You're very strange," she says. "Who are you?"

Alissa smiles absently at Stein and Max Thor.

"Do you think so?"

Stein looks happy. Elisabeth suddenly sees the two men at the window.

"Oh. There was someone there," she says.

"No. They've only just come."

Silence.

"You're always alone," Alissa says.

"People don't talk to one another here."

"What about you? Would you have spoken to me if I hadn't spoken to you?"

"No." Elisabeth smiles. "I'm rather shy. And then I'm not bored—I take too much medicine to get bored. Oh, the time goes quite fast. Not much longer now . . ."

Alissa is silent. Elisabeth Alione looks toward the windows. Stein and Max Thor are no longer there: they are in the grounds now.

"How long?"

"A week . . . My husband's the one who's bored . . .

41

He brings my daughter to see me on Sundays. She was here yesterday."

"I saw her. Quite grown-up."

"Fourteen and a half. She's not a bit like me."

"You're wrong. She still looks like you."

"What do you mean?"

"I mean . . . people have it all wrong about resemblance. She walks like you. She looked at the tennis courts the way you did when you were crying."

Elisabeth looks down at the ground.

"Oh," she says, "that was nothing. I was just being childish. It was because of Anita. I miss her."

"I don't have any children yet," Alissa says. "I haven't been married long."

"Oh"—she looks at Alissa covertly—"you've got plenty of time. Is your husband here?"

"Yes. He's been here on his own. His table's on the far side of the dining room, to the left. Do you know who I mean?"

"With glasses? Not all that young? . . . I mean——"

"That's right. I could be his daughter."

Elisabeth Alione tries to remember.

"But he's been here a long time, hasn't he?"

"Nine days. He must have arrived a couple of days after you."

"I'm getting mixed up then . . . Is he the one who looks rather sad?"

"When he's not talking, yes. He's a Jew. Can you tell when someone's a Jew?"

"I'm not very good at it. But my husband can tell at once, even when . . ."

She stops, realizing the danger.

"Can he? There's another man with him. Stein. He's a Jew too. You must be mixing them up."

Alissa smiles at her. She is reassured.

"I've just been staying with my parents," Alissa explains. "I came to pick him up. We're going away on vacation in a few days. Come on, just come for a stroll around the grounds."

They get up.

"Where are you going for your vacation?" Elisabeth Alione asks.

"We never know in advance," Alissa says.

They reach the tennis courts. Stein is coming down the steps of the hotel.

"Why didn't you take the advice of the second doctor?" Alissa asks.

Elisabeth starts and gives a little cry.

"Oh, you've guessed there was something," she says.

They come to the steps. Stein is waiting for them.

"This is Stein," Alissa says. "Elisabeth Alione."

"We were looking for you to go for a walk in the forest," Stein says.

Max Thor now comes down the steps. Slowly, his eyes lowered. Alissa and Stein watch him approach.

"Let me introduce my husband," Alissa says. "Max Thor. Elisabeth Alione."

Elisabeth doesn't notice anything, neither the icy hand nor the pallor. She tries to remember, but can't.

"I'd got you mixed up," she says, smiling.

"Let's go into the forest," Alissa says.

She starts to go, followed by Stein. Max Thor doesn't appear to have heard. Elisabeth Alione waits. Then

Max Thor moves toward Alissa as if to stop her. But
Alissa has already set off.

Then all three turn toward Elisabeth Alione. She
hasn't moved.

"Come along," Alissa says.

"Well . . ."

"Madame Alione's afraid of the forest," says Alissa.

"In that case we can stay in the grounds," Max Thor
says.

Alissa comes back to Elisabeth and smiles at her.

"Choose," she says.

"I don't mind going into the forest," she says.

The two women set out, preceded by Stein and Max
Thor.

"Let's stay in the grounds," Elisabeth Alione says.

Silence.

"As you like," Alissa says.

Silence. They retrace their steps.

"To go back to what we were saying," Stein says.
"Total destruction."

Night in the grounds of the hotel. Bright light.

Alissa is lying on the grass. Max Thor is standing over
her. They are alone.

"Middle class background," Alissa says. "The husband probably has his own business. She must have
married very young and had the daughter right away.
They've gone on living in the Dauphine. He took over
the father's business. She's terrified."

Alissa gets up.

They look at each other.

"According to her she's terrified at the thought of being abandoned. She trots out the story about the baby who died, too. But there must have been something else, something serious."

"Let's go."

"No."

" 'The man in the bookshop tells me what to buy. He knows me, he knows the sort of books I like. My husband only reads science. He doesn't like novels, the books he reads are very difficult . . . Oh, it's not that I don't like reading . . . but at the moment . . . I sleep . . ' "

He is silent.

" 'I'm afraid,' " Alissa goes on. " 'Afraid of being abandoned, afraid of the future, afraid of loving, of violence, of numbers, of the unknown, of hunger, of poverty, of the truth.' "

"You're insane, Alissa. Insane."

"I surprise myself too," says Alissa.

Silence.

"When she says, 'I sleep,' I see her sleeping and you watching her."

"Only me?"

"No."

Silence.

Alissa looks around.

"Where's Stein?"

"He'll be here. Come up to the room."

"I'm waiting for Stein."

"We'll leave tomorrow, Alissa."

"That's not possible. We're meeting Elisabeth Alione after her nap."

"Will we go into the forest?"

"No. We'll stay in the grounds."

Stein emerges from them.

"Your hair," he says.

He touches it. It has been cut.

"It was so beautiful," says Stein.

"Too beautiful."

He thinks.

"Has he noticed?" he says, pointing to Max Thor.

"He hasn't said anything yet. I cut it myself. It was lying all over the bathroom floor. He must have stepped on it."

"I did exclaim," Max Thor says.

"I heard him exclaim. But he didn't say anything. I thought you cried out for some other reason."

Stein takes her in his arms.

"For what reason?" Max Thor asks.

"Impatience," Alissa says.

Silence.

"Come over here, Alissa," Stein says.

"Yes. What will become of us?"

"I've no idea."

"We've no idea," Max Thor says.

Alissa Thor speaks with her head buried in Stein's arms.

"She's getting used to us. She said, 'M. Stein's a man who inspires confidence.' "

They laugh.

"What did she say about him?" Stein says, pointing to Max Thor.

"Nothing. She talked about leaving. She won't leave

the grounds now; she says she's expecting her husband
to telephone."

They are walking round the tennis courts. The balcony of their room is lit up.

"We could go into the forest with her," Stein says.

"No," Max Thor cries.

"We've only got three days left," says Alissa. "Three
nights."

They stop.

"He wants to go. He says so, Stein."

"Play-acting," Stein says.

"I can't go now," Alissa says.

"Come up to the room," Max Thor says.

Day in the grounds.

Elisabeth Alione is seated at a table. Alissa Thor is
beside her.

"Both doctors said I ought to go away," Elisabeth
Alione says. "I kept crying all the time. I couldn't even
have said why."

She smiles at Alissa.

"There I am talking about it again . . . I suppose I
can't help myself."

"Why did they insist on your being alone? If you
weren't a . . . strong sort of person, it might have been
rather dangerous, mightn't it?"

Elisabeth lowers her eyes and is wary. For the first
time.

"I'm not a strong person." She looks at her. "You're
wrong there."

"Is that what you say?"

Elisabeth's eyes are moving about again. There is a distant warning in her voice.

"That's what the people around me say. And I agree."

"But who?"

"Oh . . . the doctors . . . and my husband."

"A woman in your position—mentally . . . and physically—is very vulnerable. Things could happen to her that normally wouldn't. Didn't they tell you that?"

"I don't understand," Elisabeth Alione says, after a pause.

"Other women . . . not you . . . might get into some scrape or other . . ."

Alissa laughs. So does Elisabeth.

"What an idea! Oh no, not me!"

They are silent.

"They're late," says Alissa. "We said five o'clock."

"I've kept you from having your walk," Elisabeth Alione says apologetically. "I'm sorry. Especially as my husband didn't phone."

"Is it always your husband who phones?"

Elisabeth flushes.

"Yes. Well . . . someone else did call once when I first came, but I hung up."

"Good heavens," Alissa says, smiling.

"It's all over now." She turns to Alissa. "We're very different."

"Yes. I'm happy with my husband too, but probably in a different way."

"How?"

They look at each other. Alissa doesn't answer.

48

"Max Thor's a writer, isn't he?"

Does she notice Alissa start? No.

"Well, he's in the process of becoming one . . . but no, he isn't one yet . . . What makes you ask?"

Elisabeth smiles.

"I don't know . . . that's what I'd have thought."

"He's a professor. I was one of his students."

"Who is Stein?" Elisabeth Alione asks timidly.

"I can't talk about Stein," Alissa says.

"I see."

"No, you don't."

Elisabeth has started to tremble.

"Oh, please excuse me," Alissa says. "I'm sorry."

"It's nothing. You're very blunt."

"It's the thought of Stein," says Alissa. "It was just the thought of Stein's existence."

Here come the two men. They bow.

"We're late."

"Not very."

"How was the view?" Elisabeth Alione asks.

"We couldn't find the place," Max Thor says.

They sit down. Alissa deals the cards.

"Stein leads," she says.

Stein puts down a card.

"Did you get your phone call?" Max Thor asks.

"No. I'm so sorry."

"We've been talking about love," Alissa says.

Silence.

"Your turn, Mr. Thor."

"Sorry. How are you feeling?"

"Better," Elisabeth Alione says. "I don't sleep so much. I could almost go home. It's Alissa's turn."

49

"Don't you like it here?" asks Max Thor.

"Oh, it's all right, but . . ."

Stein says nothing.

"Why don't you phone and ask your husband to come get you?"

"He'd only say the doctor gave strict orders. And that the three weeks will be up in three days."

"And does that seem so long?"

They don't wait for an answer. They are intent on their cards, especially Stein.

"Well . . . no . . . But you're leaving soon too, aren't you?"

"In a few days," Max Thor says. "Aren't you going to play?"

"Sorry."

"I don't know Grenoble," Stein says.

"I'm going to lose," says Alissa. "I think I'm going to lose."

"What do you usually do in the summer?"

"When my daughter was little we used to go to Brittany. Now we go to the South."

Silence.

"I'd like to know Anita," Alissa says.

"So would I," says Stein. "My turn to play?"

"Yes."

They are peaceful.

"She's difficult," Elisabeth Alione says. "She's going through an awkward phase. But it's her age. It'll pass. She's rude . . ."

"Rude?" Max Thor says.

"Yes." She smiles. "Especially to me. She wouldn't

work last year. But her father put his foot down and this year it's much better. I think it's Max Thor's turn to play."

"Sorry."

"What did her father do?" asks Alissa.

"Oh . . ." She is embarrassed. "He wouldn't let her go out for a while. That's all."

Silence. They go on playing.

"You're very good at cards," Max Thor says.

"We play sometimes at Grenoble. Just among friends."

"On Sunday afternoon?" Alissa asks.

"That's right." She smiles. "That's what people do in the provinces."

Silence. They concentrate on the game. Elisabeth watches them with amazement. She plays almost absent-mindedly.

"Go on," she says to Stein. "Your trick."

"Sorry. Alissa's deal?"

"No. Yours. You do have a strange way of . . ." She smiles. "I suppose you don't play very often?"

"Well . . . ," Alissa says. Her thoughts wander. "What's Anita like?"

The answer doesn't come at once.

"A very affectionate child, really. I expect she'll suffer. But people are bad judges of their own children."

Silence. They go on playing. Elisabeth, though she says nothing, is more and more astonished.

"Do all your family live in Grenoble?" Max Thor asks.

"Yes. My mother's still alive." She says to Stein:

"Yes, your turn to play. I have a sister too. We live on the outskirts, not in Grenoble itself. The house is on the Isère. . . . It's a river as well as a department."

"Near the factory?" Alissa asks.

"Yes . . . How did you know?"

"I just guessed."

"Alissa's traveled a lot," Stein says. "Go on, it's your turn."

"Sorry," Max Thor says. "I expect you go to Paris every year?"

"Yes. Nearly every year. In October."

Silence. Elisabeth deals deftly. They watch her.

"The automobile show's in October," Stein says.

"Yes . . . but we go to the theater too. Oh, I know . . ." No one reacts. "I don't really like Paris."

Silence.

"All our plans are changed this year," says Alissa. "We still don't know where to go. It's Stein's turn to play."

"Sorry." He plays. "There."

"My trick," Elisabeth Alione says. "And normally I always lose. Do you usually go to the seashore?"

"No," Stein says.

"We pass by the beaches every summer," Max Thor says. "But we don't stop."

She stops playing. She looks suddenly uneasy.

"So . . . so you've known each other a long time?"

"Four days," Alissa says. "It's boring—the beach every morning and every afternoon. Don't you think so?"

"I don't understand," Elisabeth Alione murmurs.
Silence.

"Perhaps you'd rather stop playing?" Max Thor says.

52

"Sorry. I suppose you go abroad?"

"Usually," Stein says. To Alissa: "Eh?"

"Usually," Alissa says.

Elisabeth begins to giggle.

"Last year," she says, "we went to Italy with friends."

"A doctor?"

"Yes ... a doctor and his wife."

"You seem to know a lot of doctors," Alissa says.

"Yes ... quite a few ... They're interesting to talk to."

"They talk to you about yourself," Max Thor says.

"Well ... yes ..."

Silence.

"What are you laughing at?" asks Alissa.

"Sorry ... I don't know ..."

"Laugh," Stein says.

Silence. The laughter stops. But there are still traces of it in her eyes.

"My trick?" Stein asks.

"Yes," Max Thor says.

The laughter starts again. The others don't join in.

"Do you mean to say you don't even know when you've ... ?"

"Did you like Italy?"

Again the laughter seems to stop.

"Yes ... but in July ... it's terribly hot. I can't stand the heat."

"What about the food?"

The laughter begins again. But she's the only one who's laughing.

"Oh ... Oh yes ... I'm so sorry ... We went to ..."

"Laugh," Stein says.

"To?"

"Venice . . . To Venice."

The suppressed laughter spreads from her face to her hands and makes them shake. She drops some of her cards.

"We can see your hand," Stein says.

"Venice?" Max Thor says.

"Oh yes . . . we went . . . I'm so sorry . . . I don't remember . . . Oh yes . . . We went to Venice."

"Or was it Naples? Venice or Naples?"

"Or Rome?"

"Oh no . . . Venice . . . I'm sorry . . . We came back through Rome. Yes . . . Back through Rome, that's it . . ."

"It's not possible," says Stein.

They look at her gravely. She has dropped her cards.

"Have I got it wrong?"

"Completely."

They wait. They look at her.

The laughter starts.

"Whose turn to play?" Stein asks.

She laughs even louder.

"Oh . . . there's no point in trying to play . . ."

"In other words," Alissa says, "Stein doesn't know how to play cards."

"No . . . He hasn't got the slightest idea . . ."

Laughter, stronger still.

"Nor do you two . . ."

"Nor do we," Max Thor says.

She laughs. She is still the only one laughing.

"It was a good game," Stein says.

He puts down his cards. So does Alissa, then Max
Thor. Elisabeth laughs. They look at her.

"Elisabeth Villeneuve," Stein says.

The laughter becomes intermittent. She looks at each
of them in turn. Fear comes into her eyes.

The laughter stops.

Dusk in the grounds.

"Good," Max Thor says.

Elisabeth Alione has just played. She's managed to
get the croquet ball through the wicket.

"Yes," she says. "I don't know how I did it."

"Why do you always think you can't do things?"

She smiles. So do Alissa and Stein. They are standing
with mallets in their hands. They don't say anything.

"Your turn again," Max Thor says.

Elisabeth plays very carefully. She misses the wicket.
She straightens up looking absolutely delighted.

"You see," she says.

Max Thor bends down and puts the ball back where
it was. Alissa and Stein watch the other two.

"Try again," Max Thor says.

Elisabeth Alione takes fright.

"I can't," she says. "What about Alissa?"

Alissa stands silent beside Stein. Elisabeth doesn't
meet her eye.

"Alissa and Stein are thinking about something else,"
says Max Thor. "Look at them."

Elisabeth Alione hesitates.

"I can't," she says.

"Cheat," orders Max Thor. "I want you to."

55

Elisabeth Alione plays and misses the wicket. Again she is absolutely delighted.

"I told you so," she says.

"Did you do it purposely?"

"No, I didn't—really I didn't."

She looks at Alissa and Stein.

"Try again," Alissa says softly.

Elisabeth is flustered. Max Thor picks up the ball and puts it back in front of the wicket. Elisabeth plays and misses the wicket. She drops her mallet. And doesn't pick it up. Nor does Max Thor.

"My husband's coming to get me tomorrow," she says.

Silence.

"We've lost the game," Elisabeth Alione says.

Silence.

"Were we really playing?" Alissa asks at last. "I didn't think it was meant to count."

Alissa sits down and looks at them.

"What's the matter?" she asks.

"I'm leaving tomorrow," Elisabeth Alione says. "I just said so."

Max Thor has sat down too.

"I was wrong. My husband said he'd come and get me right away. Actually, I haven't been nearly so bored here since I met you. I was almost disappointed when he said he'd come."

She sits down too, and looks at them furtively.

"You've been very kind to me. He's coming tomorrow morning."

They are silent.

"If you like," she says, "we could go for a walk now.

56

We could go in the forest . . . You seemed very anxious to."

"Why did you telephone?" Alissa asks softly.

Elisabeth Alione's face grows calm again.

"To see if he'd agree, I suppose . . . I don't really know."

"Did you tell him about us?" Max Thor asks.

"No."

"There, you see," Alissa says, smiling. "You hide things from him. From the man you love."

Elisabeth Alione gives a little start.

"Oh, but it's not hiding things not to tell him that . . ."

"What do you mean?"

"People one meets in hotels . . ."

"Where else does one meet them?" says Max Thor. He says it gently. She doesn't understand.

"He'll probably never meet you . . . so there was no reason why I should tell him . . ."

"Who knows?" Alissa says.

"There'd be no point. I don't think you'd like each other . . . No, I don't think so . . . You're too different . . ."

"What did you say on the phone to make him come?"

"I don't really know myself. I said I'd stopped taking sleeping tablets . . ." She hesitates. "I mentioned you just vaguely. I said I played cards with some of the other people here. That's all. I didn't actually ask him to come right away . . . But I realized he suddenly missed me . . . Whereas . . ."

They are silent. Max Thor has taken off his glasses and seems to be resting.

"I must go in. I have to pack," Elisabeth Alione says.

The tennis players are back. The balls swish in the heat.

"I'll help you," Alissa says. "You've got plenty of time."

Alissa gets up, and she and Stein move slowly and evenly, as if dancing, away across the grounds. The other two watch them.

"Where are they going?" Elisabeth Alione asks.

"Into the forest, I expect," Max Thor says, smiling.

"I don't understand . . ."

"We're Alissa's lovers. Don't try to understand."

She thinks this over. And begins to tremble.

"Don't you think I'll ever be able to?"

"It doesn't matter," Max Thor says. He puts his glasses on again and looks at her.

"What is it?" she asks.

"I love Alissa desperately," Max Thor says.

Silence. She looks into his eyes.

"Supposing I tried to understand . . ." Elisabeth Alione says.

"I'd like to understand you," he says. "Love you."

She doesn't answer.

Silence.

"What was that book you never read?" Max Thor says.

"Oh yes, I must go and get it"—she makes a little grimace—"Oh, how I dislike reading."

"Why pretend to then?" He laughs. "No one else reads."

"When you're on your own . . . you do it to . . . to keep up appearances . . . or . . ." She smiles at him. "Where are they?"

"They can't be far. But don't go counting on Alissa to help you pack."

"I know."

She can't take her eyes off the far side of the grounds.

"Is your husband coming tonight?"

"No, tomorrow. At noon, he said. Do you think they're listening?"

"Maybe."

She comes closer, her face slightly drawn.

"The book doesn't belong to me. I have to give it back. But perhaps you'd like it?"

"No."

She comes nearer, still looking across the grounds.

"What's going to become of you?" he says.

She looks at him.

"What do you mean? . . . Oh . . . The same as before . . ."

"Sure?"

She goes on looking at him.

"Here comes Stein," Max Thor says. "We're leaving tomorrow morning."

"I'm frightened," Elisabeth Alione says. "I'm frightened of Alissa. Where is she?"

She looks at him, waiting.

"We've nothing to say to one another," says Max Thor. "Nothing."

She doesn't move. He doesn't speak. She goes off. He doesn't turn around. Stein approaches.

"The woman I've been looking for here so long," Stein says, "is Alissa."

Brilliant weather. Light and sun in the dining room. In the mirrors.

"We may meet again some day. Who knows?" Alissa says.

Elisabeth and Alissa are sitting in the shade near the armchairs.

"We live in an out-of-the-way place. You have to make a special trip."

"We could make a special trip," Alissa says.

She goes over to the bay windows.

"They're watching the tennis match," she says. "Waiting for us."

She comes back to Elisabeth Alione and sits down.

"You've made a great impression on us."

"Why?"

Alissa makes a negative gesture.

"Don't bother," Elisabeth Alione says. "I probably wouldn't understand even if you told me. I don't understand some things."

"That first doctor," says Alissa. "Did he talk to you like this?"

Elisabeth Alione gets up and goes and looks out into the grounds.

"He wrote," she says. "Out of the blue he wrote me a letter. That's all."

"Was there trouble?"

"He tried to . . . He's left Grenoble now. They said it was because of me. They said horrible things. My husband was very upset. But fortunately he trusts me."

She's come back into the shade.

"It was about the middle of my pregnancy. I'd been ill and he came to see me. He was young, he'd only been in Grenoble a couple of years. My husband was away. He got into the habit of coming. And . . ."

She stops.

"Did they say he'd killed the baby?"

"Yes. They said if it hadn't been for him my little girl . . ." She stops. "It isn't true. The baby was dead before it was born." The last words are a cry.

She waits.

"It was after the confinement that I showed my husband the letter. And it was when he found out I'd done that that he realized . . . nothing would come of it, and tried to kill himself."

"How did he find out you showed him the letter?"

"My husband went to see him. Or wrote. I'll never know which."

Alissa says nothing. Elisabeth Alione is uneasy.

"You do believe me?"

"Yes."

Elisabeth Alione sits up and looks at Alissa questioningly.

"You see, I'm the sort of person who's afraid of everything. My husband's quite different. I'm lost without him . . ."

She comes closer.

"What have you got against me?"

"Nothing," Alissa says softly. "I'm just thinking about what you told me. It was because you showed your husband the letter that you were ill. You're ill because of what you did."

She gets up.

"What's the matter?" Elisabeth Alione asks.

"Disgust," says Alissa. "Disgust."

Elisabeth Alione gives a cry.

"Do you want to make me desperate?"

Alissa smiles at her.

"Yes. Don't say any more."

"No, let's not talk any more."

"It's too late," says Alissa.

"For what?"

"To kill you." She smiles. "It's too late."

Silence.

Alissa draws nearer to Elisabeth Alione.

"You've liked being with us, haven't you?"

Elisabeth lets her approach without answering.

"Is that why you phoned for your husband to come?"

"I love my husband, I think."

Alissa smiles.

"It's fascinating to see the way you live," she says. "Fascinating and terrible."

"I realized," Elisabeth Alione says softly, "you were only interested in me because of . . . that. And that perhaps you were right."

"What do you mean, 'that'?"

Elisabeth makes a gesture signifying she doesn't know. Alissa takes her by the shoulders.

Elisabeth turns. They are both reflected in the mirror.

"Who is it that makes you think of him?" Alissa asks in the mirror. "Of the doctor?"

"Stein, perhaps."

"Look," says Alissa.

Silence. Their heads are close together.

"We're alike," says Alissa. "We'd love Stein if it were possible to love."

"I didn't say . . ." Elisabeth protests softly.

"You meant to say Max Thor," says Alissa. "And you said Stein. You can't even say what you mean."

"No."

They look at one another in the mirror and smile.

"How beautiful you are," Elisabeth says.

"We're women," Alissa says. "Look."

They go on looking at themselves. Then Elisabeth puts her head against Alissa's. Alissa's hand is on Elisabeth Alione's skin, on her shoulder.

"I think we look alike," Alissa murmurs. "Don't you think so? We're the same height."

They smile.

"So we are."

Alissa slides Elisabeth's sleeve off her shoulder.

". . . the same skin," she goes on. "The same color skin."

"Perhaps . . ."

"Look . . . the shape of the mouth . . . the hair."

"Why did you cut it? I was so sorry . . ."

"To look more like you."

"Such lovely hair . . . I didn't say anything, but . . ."

"Why?"

She would never have said it. Does she know she is saying it now?

"I knew you'd cut it because of me."

Alissa takes hold of Elisabeth Alione's hair and puts her face where she wants it—beside her own.

"We look very much alike," Alissa says. "How strange."

"You're younger than I am . . . and more intelligent . . ."

"Not just now," Alissa says.

Alissa looks at Elisabeth Alione's clothed body in the glass.

"I love and desire you," Alissa says.

Elisabeth Alione doesn't move. She shuts her eyes.

"You're insane," she murmurs.

"Too bad," Alissa says.

Elisabeth Alione suddenly moves away. Alissa goes over to the bay windows.

Silence.

"Your husband's just arrived," she says. "He's looking for you outside. Your daughter isn't with him."

Elisabeth Alione doesn't move.

"And the others? Where are they?" she asks.

"Watching him. They recognize him." She turns. "What is it you're afraid of?"

"I'm not afraid."

Alissa looks out into the grounds again. Elisabeth still stands motionless.

"They're coming in so as not to have to see him," Alissa says. "Disgust, I suppose. There, they've come in. I suppose they'll come in here unless they go through to the road."

Elisabeth doesn't answer.

"We knew each other as children," she says. "Our families were friends."

Alissa repeats softly:

" 'We knew each other as children. Our families were friends.' "

Silence.

"If you'd loved him, if you'd loved him once, just once in your life, you'd have loved the others," Alissa says. "Stein and Max Thor."

"I don't understand . . ." Elisabeth says, "but . . ."

"It'll happen other times," Alissa says, "later. And it won't be you or them. Pay no attention to what I say."

"Stein says you're insane," Elisabeth says.

"Stein will say anything."

Alissa laughs. She turns back into the room and comes over.

"The only thing that will ever have happened to you . . ." she says.

"Is you," Elisabeth says. "You, Alissa."

"Wrong again," Alissa says. "But let's go down."

Elisabeth doesn't move.

"We're having lunch together. Didn't you know?"

"Whose idea was that?"

"Stein's," Alissa says.

Stein comes in.

"Your husband's waiting for you," he says to Elisabeth Alione, "by the tennis courts. We're all to meet in ten minutes."

"But I don't understand," she says.

"It's irrevocable now," Stein says, smiling. "Your husband's agreed."

She goes out. Stein takes Alissa in his arms.

"Love . . . my love," he says.

"Stein," says Alissa.

"Last night I spoke your name."

"In your sleep."

"Yes. Alissa. Your name woke me up. I was outside. I looked in. You were both asleep. The room was in a mess. You were asleep on the floor and he had come and gone to sleep beside you. You'd forgotten to turn off the light."

"We had?"

"Yes."

And now Max Thor is here.

"We don't know where to go," he says, "with *him* out there."

Alissa stands in front of Max Thor and looks straight at him.

"Last night," she says, "in your sleep, you spoke her name. Elisa."

"I don't remember," Max Thor says. "I don't remember."

Alissa goes over to Stein.

"Tell him, Stein."

"You spoke her name," says Stein. "Elisa."

"How did I say it?"

"Tenderly and longingly," Stein says. "Elisa."

Silence.

Max Thor to Alissa:

"Perhaps I said Alissa and you misunderstood?"

"No," says Alissa. "Remember your dream."

Silence.

"I think it was in the hotel grounds," Max Thor says slowly. "She must have been asleep. I stood there watching her. Yes . . . that's it . . ."

He is silent.

Stein to Max Thor:

"And she said, 'Oh, it's you . . .'?"

" 'I wasn't really asleep'? 'I was only pretending'? 'Did you realize?'?"

"For days I've been pretending'? 'For days I've been sleeping'? 'Ten days'?"

"Perhaps," Max Thor says. He speaks the name: "Elisa."

"Yes. You must have been calling her when you spoke her name."

Silence.

"I answered you," Alissa says. "But you were so sound asleep you didn't hear."

Max Thor goes over to the bay windows. The other two join him.

"What could come of it?" Stein asks.

"Desire," Max Thor says. "In such circumstances, desire."

Alissa turns to Stein.

"Sometimes," she says, "he doesn't understand . . ."

"It doesn't matter," Stein says.

"Yes," says Max Thor. "It doesn't matter now."

Silence. They look out of the window at invisible guests. Among them Elisabeth Alione and her husband.

Silence.

"How can one live?" Alissa cries softly.

The sun is shining brightly.

"Hasn't the daughter come?" Max Thor asks.

"She asked him not to bring her today."

"Fine," Stein says. "She's . . ."

"Here they come," Max Thor says.

They are coming round by the tennis courts to the hotel entrance.

"How can one live?" Alissa breathes.

"What will become of us?" Stein asks.

The Aliones have come into the dining room.

"Look how she's trembling," Max Thor says.

The two groups move toward each other.

They are close enough to exchange greetings.

"Bernard Alione," Elisabeth breathes. "Alissa."

"Stein."

"Max Thor."

Bernard Alione looks at Alissa. There is a silence.

"Oh," he says. "So you're Alissa? She was just telling me about you."

"What did she say?" Stein asks.

"Oh, nothing . . ." Bernard Alione says, smiling.

They move toward their table.

Brilliant weather. The blinds have been lowered. Sunday.

They are having lunch.

"We'll be in Grenoble by about five," Bernard Alione says.

"Such marvelous weather," Alissa says. "It's a pity to leave today."

"All good things come to an end . . . I'm very glad to have met you . . . Elisabeth wasn't as bored as she might have been, because of you . . . the last few days, I mean."

"She wasn't bored even before we met."

"A little bit, in the evening," Elisabeth Alione says.

Silence. Elisabeth, in black, in the blue shade of the blinds, her back to the windows, stares in front of her like someone asleep.

"She was asleep," Alissa says.

Bernard Alione smiles, opens up.

"Elisabeth has never been able to bear being alone . . . under any circumstances . . . Every time I had to go away . . . and I have to because of my work . . . Every time there was a scene"—he smiles at her—"Wasn't there, Elisa?"

68

"Elisa," Max Thor murmurs.

"I'm going mad," Elisabeth Alione says softly.

"And is she often?" Alissa asks. "Alone, I mean?"

"You mean, without me? Yes, quite often . . . But one of the family always comes." He smiles at Alissa. "Still, it's never too late."

They don't understand.

"It was her idea to come here," Bernard Alione says. "Hers alone. Just like that." He almost laughs. "She realized she ought to make the effort."

They look at her, asleep at the table, her eyes wide open. She gives a childlike toss of the head, calling for silence concerning her life.

"I was tired," she says.

Her voice is distant, exhausted. She has stopped eating. So has Max Thor.

"Were you bored here?" Max Thor asks.

She hesitates.

"No," she says, "no." She tries to think. "I don't think so."

"When boredom takes a certain form . . ." Stein says. Then stops.

"Yes?" says Bernard Alione. "You were going to say something interesting. What . . . what form were you thinking of?"

"When it's become part of a timetable, say, you don't notice it," says Stein. "And if you don't notice it, don't give it a name, it can take some curious turns."

"There's something in what you say," Bernard Alione says.

"There is," Stein says.

Bernard Alione stops eating.

"What turns . . . for example?" he asks.

Stein looks at Elisabeth Alione and considers. Then forgets.

"Impossible to predict," he says.

Stein and Elisabeth Alione look at each other in silence.

"Quite impossible," he murmurs. "What's going to become of you?"

"What?" asks Bernard Alione.

"Don't pay any attention to what Stein says," Alissa says.

Silence. Bernard Alione looks at them.

"Who are you?" he asks.

"German Jews," Alissa says.

"That's not what I . . . that's not the point . . ."

"I think it must have been," Max Thor says gently. Silence.

"Elisabeth's not eating," Bernard Alione says.

"Perhaps she feels sick," Alissa says.

Elisabeth doesn't move. She sits looking into her lap.

"What's going on?" Bernard Alione says.

"We all feel the same," says Stein. "All four of us." Silence.

Elisabeth gets up and goes out. They watch her through the bay window. With her leisurely gait she walks across the grounds and disappears down the path that leads to the gate into the forest.

"She's gone to be sick," Alissa says.

Silence. Bernard Alione has begun to eat again, then notices he is the only one.

"I'm the only one eating . . ."

70

"Go on," Max Thor says. "It doesn't matter."

But Bernard Alione stops eating and looks at the other three. They are all quite calm.

"We'll soon be going away to the seashore, and then Elisabeth will be perfectly all right. I thought I'd find her in better shape today. She still needs rest."

They say nothing. They look at him and say nothing.

"I expect she told you about it . . . a stupid accident . . ."

No reaction from anyone.

"It was really more of an emotional shock for her than anything . . . A woman feels that sort of thing as a kind of failure. We men can't really understand . . ."

He fidgets on his chair, gets up, looks around.

"Yes . . . well . . . time we were off . . . I'll go and find her . . . By the time the luggage gets downstairs . . ."

He looks out at the grounds.

". . . and I've paid the bill . . ."

Silence.

"Where are you going for your vacation?"

This reassures him.

"Leucate. Perhaps you know it? I'm interested in the Languedoc development scheme"—he smiles—"I'm not like my wife, I can't just spend my vacation twiddling my thumbs . . ."

He smiles. Alissa has turned to Stein.

"Leucate," Alissa says.

Silence. Bernard Alione may not have heard. He smiles. He has sat down again.

"You've seen more of her than I have recently," he says. "What is it that . . . ?"

"Fear," Stein says.

Bernard Alione is confused by the gentle way in which they are looking at him.

"It will be terrible," Stein murmurs softly. "Frightful." He looks at Bernard Alione. "And she's beginning to realize."

"Who are you talking about?"

"Elisabeth Alione."

Bernard Alione gets up. No one does anything to stop him. He sits down again and gives a brief laugh.

"I didn't realize . . . You're all crazy," he says. "Now I see."

Silence. He is sitting a little way away from the table now. He looks at Alissa. Her eyes are deep blue, happy and gentle.

"That illness," she asks. "That doctor."

"Yes," Stein says. "That doctor who died."

"He didn't die," Bernard Alione cries.

Silence.

"I don't understand," Bernard Alione says. "Did she tell you about . . . about the accident?"

"What death did he choose?" Max Thor asks.

Silence. The blinds are raised with a harsh grating noise. The sky has grown overcast.

"He didn't die," says Bernard Alione softly. "Put that idea out of your heads . . . As far as Elisa was concerned, it was just the death of the little girl . . . The rest . . . No . . . The idea!"

Suddenly he understands and his voice goes blank.

"Has she told you about us?" Max Thor asks.

"Not yet."

"We've been with her all the time for the last four days."

72

Bernard Alione doesn't answer. He jumps up, goes over to the window and calls her. A long cry:

"Elisabeth."

No answer. He turns round and looks at them.

"It's no use calling," Stein says.

"Don't pay any attention to what Stein says," says Alissa. "She's coming."

Bernard Alione sits down and turns towards the dining room. It is empty.

"They're all out for the day," Max Thor explains. He smiles at Bernard Alione. "Has she told you about us?"

Bernard Alione starts to gabble.

"No, but she will . . . I know she will . . . You must have noticed, she's very reserved . . . for no reason at all . . . even with me, and I'm her husband."

"When she went away," says Alissa, "when she suggested coming to stay here, didn't she tell you why?"

"Why don't you mind your own business?" Bernard Alione cries weakly.

"What did she tell you?" Stein says.

Alissa turns to Stein.

"She must have told him she needed to be alone for a while. Long enough to forget about the doctor."

"Yes," Stein says. "Yes, that must be it."

"And now," says Max Thor, "she *has* forgotten."

Silence. Alissa has taken Stein's hand and kisses it without speaking. Max Thor looks out into the grounds. Bernard Alione is quite still now.

"Here she is," Max Thor says.

She is coming toward them under the clouded sky. Very slowly. She stops. Then walks on. Bernard Alione doesn't watch her coming.

73

"Where did you find her?" Max Thor asks.

"They knew each other as children," Alissa recites. "Their families were friends."

Silence. The others continue to watch her approaching. She has stopped, facing the tennis courts. She is twisting some blades of grass in her fingers.

"You're all remarkably interested in her," Bernard Alione says.

"Yes."

"Might one inquire why?"—his voice is stronger again.

"Literary reasons," Stein says, laughing.

He goes on laughing. Alissa watches him, enchanted.

"So my wife's a character in a novel?" Bernard Alione says.

He sneers. But his voice is still strained in spite of his efforts.

"A perfect one," Max Thor answers.

"Is it you . . .?" Bernard Alione says.

He points to Max Thor.

"Is it Monsieur . . . Thor who's the author?"

"No," says Max Thor.

"I don't see what you could find to say about her. Of course I know novels don't tell stories any more . . . That's why I hardly ever read them . . . That's why . . ."

He looks at them. They are serious now, not listening to him. Elisabeth is coming across the dining room.

She sits down. Her eyes are still wide open but as if in sleep.

Silence.

"Were you sick?" Alissa asks.

Elisabeth has difficulty forming her words.

74

"Yes."

"What was it like?"

Elisabeth thinks it over. She smiles.

"Pleasant," she says.

"Fine," Stein says. "Fine."

Silence. Bernard Alione looks at his wife. She has put the grass on the table and is looking at it.

"I was worried," he said. "Are you sure it isn't all those drugs?"

"I've stopped taking them."

"Yes, she's stopped taking them," Max Thor says. He addresses Elisabeth Alione. "But did you sleep?"

"No."

Silence. Elisabeth raises her head and looks straight into Alissa's blue eyes.

"Have you noticed her eyes?" she asks Bernard Alione.

"Yes."

Silence.

"What do you make in your factory?" Stein asks.

Bernard Alione tears his eyes away from Alissa's and looks round at the four faces awaiting his answer. He begins to tremble.

"Canned food," he mumbles.

Silence.

"I think I'm going to be sick again," Elisabeth Alione says.

"Fine," Stein says. "Fine."

"We must go," Bernard Alione mutters. He doesn't move.

"You know," Alissa says with incomparable gentleness, "you know, we could love you too."

"Really love you," Stein says.

"Yes," says Max Thor. "We could."

Silence. Elisabeth has moved. She looks at her husband, who sits with bowed head. She has started to tremble.

"We must go," she reminds him gently.

Alissa and Stein have drawn together, unmindful of the others.

"She's said it," Stein says.

"Yes. They must go."

Silence. Alissa doesn't move. Now it is Elisabeth Alione's eyes that try to get some hold on the smooth wall of their faces. She fails.

"Don't be cross with her," Max Thor says to Bernard Alione. "Don't be cross with her because we're what we are."

"He won't be cross with me," she says. "He knows you can't be otherwise." She turns to Bernard Alione. "Don't you?"

No answer. Head bowed, he waits.

"What about you?" he asks. "What do you teach?"

"History," Max Thor says. "History of the future."

Silence. Bernard Alione gazes at Max Thor, motionless. His voice is unrecognizable now.

"Is it very different?" he asks.

"There's nothing left," Max Thor says. "So I don't say anything. The students go to sleep."

Silence. Suddenly there are gentle sobs from Elisabeth Alione.

"Are there still children?" she asks.

"Only children," Max Thor says.

She smiles through her tears. He takes her hand.

"Oh," she says. "Wonderful."

Bernard Alione, still motionless, goes on asking questions. He addresses Stein:

"What about you, Blum? What do you teach?"

"Nothing," says Max Thor. "Nothing. Neither does she."

Silence.

"Sometimes," Alissa says, "Blum teaches the Rosenfeld theory."

Bernard Alione ponders.

"Never heard of it," he says.

"Arthur Rosenfeld," Stein says. "He's dead."

"He was a child," Max Thor says.

"How old?" Elisabeth Alione wails.

"Eight," says Stein. "Alissa knew him."

"By the sea," Alissa says.

Silence. Stein and Alissa are holding hands. Max Thor points to them.

"Look at them," he says. "They're children already."

"Anything's possible," Bernard Alione says.

Alissa and Stein aren't listening. They both seem to be caught up by the same idea.

Elisabeth points to them too, in wonder.

"Her name's Alissa," she says. "The other two are her lovers."

Silence.

"She's gone," Stein says.

"Elisabeth Alione's left us," Alissa says.

Max Thor goes over to them. He too becomes oblivious of the others.

"Would you have liked to see her again?" Alissa says.

"Did she say why she left sooner than she planned? And the telephone call? Did she explain about it?"

77

"No, we'll never know."

Elisabeth Alione has relapsed into slumber. Alissa withdraws her hands from Stein's and looks toward Bernard Alione.

"She began to notice we were interested in her, you see," Alissa says. "She couldn't stand it."

He doesn't answer. Alissa gets up and wanders round the dining room. Stein watches her; he is the only one to do so. She goes over to the bay windows.

"The tennis courts are empty," she says. "So are the grounds. It seemed incredible she shouldn't have guessed."

She stands still.

"There was the beginning of . . . A sort of shudder . . . No . . . a crack . . ."

"Physical," Stein says.

"Yes."

Elisabeth Alione has looked up.

"We must go," she says.

Then Alissa goes over to Bernard Alione.

"There's no hurry," she says.

She's close to him but looks out of the bay window at the forest.

"What's the hurry?"

"No hurry," Bernard Alione says. "None at all."

She looks at him.

"Let's not separate," she says.

Elisabeth suddenly jumps up without a word.

"Come into the forest with us," says Alissa. She's speaking just to him. "Let's not separate."

"No," Elisabeth Alione cries.

"Why?" Bernard Alione asks. "Why in the forest?"

Silence.

"With me," Alissa begs.

"Why in the forest?"

He looks up, meets her blue eyes, and is silent.

"It's classified as a historical monument," Stein says.

"Just a little way," she says. "Enough to see."

"No."

"Alissa," Stein calls.

She goes and sits beside him again.

"That's not the way," Stein says.

Alissa clings to Stein.

"It's difficult. So difficult," she almost keens.

"That's not the way," Stein repeats.

Elisabeth Alione goes over to her husband. Max Thor has risen to go over to her, but stops.

"We must go now," she says.

"Yes," Max Thor says. "Go."

Bernard Alione struggles to his feet. He points to Alissa and Stein. Stein has taken Alissa's mask-like face in his hands.

"Is Alissa crying?" he asks.

"No," Stein says.

He turns her mask toward him and studies it.

"She's resting," he says.

Bernard Alione staggers slightly.

"I've drunk too much," he says. "I didn't realize."

"Fine," says Stein. "Fine."

Max Thor takes a step toward Elisabeth Alione.

"Where are you going?"

"Back."

"Where?" Alissa asks without moving.

"Here?" says Stein.

79

Bernard Alione gestures "no." Alissa has looked up and smiles at him. Max Thor and Stein smile at him too.

"She could have loved you . . . you too," she says. "If she'd been capable of loving."

Silence.

"Anything's possible," says Bernard Alione. He smiles.

"Yes."

Silence.

Alissa frees herself from Stein's grasp.

"How can you live with her?" Alissa cries.

Bernard Alione doesn't answer now.

"He doesn't live with her," Stein says.

"There won't have been anyone but us, then?"

"That's right."

Max Thor goes over to Elisabeth Alione.

"You'd been watching me for ten days," he says. "There was something about me that fascinated you, put you in a turmoil . . . something interesting . . . you couldn't make out what it was."

Bernard Alione seems not to hear anything any more.

"Yes," Elisabeth Alione says at last.

Silence. They look at her, but once more she calls down silence on her life.

"We could stay here at the hotel," Bernard Alione says. "For a day."

"No."

"As you like."

She goes out first. Bernard Alione only follows. Max Thor remains standing. Alissa and Stein, apart now, watch them.

Voices are heard:

"The luggage is down."

"Can I have the bill? Will you take a check?"

Silence.

"They're going across the grounds," Stein says.

Silence.

"They're going around by the tennis courts."

Silence.

"She disappeared first."

Dusk. The sun sinks in the grey lake of the sky.

Dusk in the hotel.

Stein is stretched out in the armchair. Alissa lies on top of him, her head on his chest.

They sleep and sleep.

Max Thor comes back into the room.

"I've told them to call us just before six," he says.

"You take N 113," Stein says without moving, "and turn off at Narbonne."

Max Thor stretches out in the other chair. He points to Alissa.

"She's resting," Stein says.

"Yes. My love."

"Yes."

Max Thor offers Stein a cigarette. Stein takes one. They talk quietly.

"Perhaps we oughtn't to have gone into the whole thing?" Max Thor says. "Elisabeth Alione?"

"It wouldn't have made any difference."

Silence.

"What could have come of it?"

Stein doesn't answer.

"Desire?" Max Thor asks. "And erosion by desire?"

"Yes. By your desire."

Silence.

"Or death by Alissa," Stein says.

Silence.

Stein smiles.

"We don't have any choice now," he says.

Silence.

"Would she have gone into the forest with Alissa?" asks Max Thor. "What do you think?"

Stein strokes Alissa's legs and presses her to him.

"She belongs to whoever wants her. She feels whatever they feel. Yes."

Silence.

"It would have taken a few more days," says Stein, "for her to yield to Alissa's desire."

"It was a strong one."

"Yes."

Silence.

"But not clear."

"No. Alissa would have found out in the forest."

Silence.

"The place they're going to is very small," says Stein. "It will be easy to find them in the evening, in the streets or in the cafes. She'll be glad to see us."

Silence.

"We'll say we've stopped in Leucate on our way to Spain. We'll say we like it and have decided to stay."

"It *is* on our way."

"Yes."

Silence.

"Let's rest," Stein says.

Silence.

"I can see it all," Max Thor says. "The square. The cafes. It's so easy."

"Yes, very. She's gentle, cheerful."

"Let's rest, Stein."

"Yes"—he points to Alissa—"she's resting."

Silence.

"She's having a wonderful sleep," says Stein.

"Yes. Our sleep."

"Yes."

Silence.

"Did you hear anything?"

"Yes. A sort of crack in the air?"

"Yes."

Silence. Alissa moans, stirs, then is still.

"She's dreaming," says Stein.

"Or did she hear it too?"

Silence.

"Someone beating a gong?"

"Sounded rather like . . ."

Silence.

"Or was she dreaming? She can't choose her own dreams?"

"No."

Silence. They smile at each other.

"Did she say something?"

Stein looks at Alissa closely, listens to her body.

"No. Her lips are parted but she isn't saying anything."

Silence.

"How old is Alissa?" asks Stein.

"Eighteen."

"And when you met her?"

"Eighteen."

Silence.

"There it is again," says Max Thor. "Muffled this time."

"Like someone hitting a tree."

"Or as if the earth trembled."

Silence.

"Let's rest, Stein."

"Yes."

Silence.

"Alissa isn't dead?"

"No. She's breathing."

They smile at each other.

"Let's rest."

Stein is still holding Alissa. Max Thor leans his head back in the chair. There is a long moment's rest. The grey lake grows darker.

Only when the darkness is almost complete can it be heard clearly. With immeasurable strength, sublime gentleness, it enters the hotel.

They laugh without moving.

"Oh," says Stein. "That was it . . ."

"Yes . . ."

Alissa doesn't move. Nor does Stein. Nor does Max Thor.

With infinite pain the music stops, begins again, stops, repeats, starts again. Stops.

"Is it coming from the forest?" Max Thor asks.

"Or from the garage. Or from the road."

The music begins again, loudly. Then stops.

"It's a long way away," says Stein.

"Perhaps some child playing with a radio?"
"Probably."
Silence. They don't move.
Then the music begins again, louder. It lasts longer this time. But stops again.
"It *is* coming from the forest," says Stein. "What pain. What immense pain. How difficult it is."
"It has so far to travel, so many barriers to get through."
"Yes. Everything."
The music begins again. This time majestically loud. It stops again.
"It's going to do it, it's going to get through the forest," Stein says. "Here it comes."
They speak in the intervals of the music, softly, so as not to wake Alissa.
"It has to fell trees, knock down walls," Stein murmurs. "But here it is."
"Nothing to worry about any more," says Max Thor. "Yes, here it is."
Yes, here it is, felling trees, knocking down walls.
They are bending over Alissa.
In her sleep Alissa's childlike mouth widens in pure laughter.
They laugh to see her laugh.
"Music to the name of Stein," she says.

Note for Performance

For the theater, a single set consisting of the hotel dining room and the grounds outside, separated by a window that can be raised and lowered.

An abstract décor would be best.

The whole depth of the stage should be used. A plain tarpaulin backcloth could represent the forest.

No attempt should be made to represent the tennis courts. Only the sound of the balls.

No need for any people but the main characters. The others can be suggested by the light falling on various objects: chaises-longues in a circle, or separate, or facing each other, empty. In the dining room, white cloths on the tables supposed to be "occupied."

The music at the end is fugue no. 15 (in some recordings 18 or 19) of J. S. Bach's "The Art of the Fugue."

The play should be performed in a medium-sized theater, preferably a modern one.

No public dress rehearsal should be held.

Alissa is of average height, petite if anything. Not childlike: she *is* a child. Very easy in her movements. Blue jeans and bare feet. Thick untidy hair, blonde or brown.

87

Stein and Max Thor are both about the same height, and both wear ordinary suits. Neither is careless in his dress.

Stein has a long rapid stride.

Max Thor walks slowly, and talks much more slowly than Stein.

Stein is transfixed with knowledge. Knowledge comes to Max Thor only through Stein and Alissa.

No one actually "cries out," even when the words are used: the words indicate an inner reaction only.

DESTRUCTION AND LANGUAGE

Many of Marguerite Duras' novels, including Destroy, She Said, *have been made into films. In the following interview, Jacques Rivette, Jean Narboni, and Mme. Duras discuss the two media and also the content of* Destroy, She Said.

An Interview with
Marguerite Duras
by Jacques Rivette
and Jean Narboni*
Translated by
Helen Lane Cumberford

I

JACQUES RIVETTE: ... it seems you want more and
more to give successive forms to each of the things—
let's not use the word stories—that you write, for instance *The Square*, which had several versions, or *La
Musica*, which also had several forms, or *L'Amante
Anglaise*. This corresponds to ...

MARGUERITE DURAS: To the desire that I always have
to tear what has gone before to pieces. *Destroy*, the
book *Destroy*, is a fragmented book from the novel-
istic point of view. I don't think there are any sentences
left in it. And there are directions that are mindful of
scripts: "sunshine," "seventh day," "heat," etc.; "in-
tense light," "dusk"—do you see what I mean? These
are usually stage directions. That is to say I would like
the material that is to be read to be as free as possible
of style; I can't read novels at all any more. Because
of the sentences. ...

RIVETTE: ... when you wrote these stage directions,

* *Cahiers du Cinéma*, November, 1969.

was the idea of a film hovering on the horizon? Or was it simply because you could only write in this form?

DURAS: I had no idea of a film, but I did have the idea of a book—how shall I put it?—of a book that could be either read or acted or filmed or, I always add, simply thrown away.

RIVETTE: In any case you had theater in mind somehow, since the last two pages of the book ...

DURAS: Yes, yes, Claude Régy was to stage it, and then I made the film first, I couldn't help it ... I believe it necessary to create things that are more and more time-saving, that can be read more quickly, that give the reader a more important role. There are ten ways to read *Destroy*; that's what I wanted. And ten ways to see it too, perhaps. But, you know, it's a book I hardly know at all. I know the film better than the book; I wrote the book very fast. There was a good scenario, called *The Chaise-Longue*, which we tried to film; but it came out of a certain kind of psychology, maybe a searching one, but psychology nonetheless; and Stein wasn't in it ...

RIVETTE: Did the scenario come before the writing of the book?

DURAS: *The Chaise-Longue*, yes. There were only three characters. Still, as a story it was obviously classical. When I found Stein, the scenario wasn't any good at all any more, and we threw the whole thing out that same day.

JEAN NARBONI: I was struck by an interesting contrast between the film and the book. The directions for the characters are very brief in the book, but a certain number of acts and gestures in the book are omitted

92

from the film: in the end, it is a sort of mechanical process that is exactly the opposite of the one whereby a bad filmmaker who adapts a book keeps the events, the facts, the physical acts and leaves out everything which would seem, on the contrary, to belong to the writing properly speaking. And here one has the impression that you took out everything that would seem to stem directly from "cinema," and that you kept what would seem to belong to the realm of literature.

DURAS: That is correct; I had a feeling that this was so. Are you thinking of any special gesture?

NARBONI: I'm thinking of several: the moment, for example, when Stein strokes Alissa's legs. In the film the only part of this passage that is left is the conversation.

DURAS: It so happens that during rehearsals I realized that it was impossible, because of Michael Lonsdale, who is gigantic. He was too important, if you like, sitting there at Alissa's feet, close to her legs. I had to keep him away from the other two, so that they wouldn't be completely overwhelmed. So it was really for practical reasons that I came to omit this gesture. I worked on this gesture—on the possibility, that is, of keeping this gesture—for a long time. I wasn't able to do so, and I'm sorry.

RIVETTE: But these were rehearsals that took place before . . .

DURAS: That took place at my house. For a month and a half.

RIVETTE: Did you rehearse everything before shooting?

DURAS: Yes.

RIVETTE: But wasn't it also true that Stein at that juncture was too much on the same plane as the other characters? Or was it just this one gesture that was impossible?

DURAS: Yes. Oh, it's very hard to say why it was impossible. It wasn't possible; it obviously wasn't possible. Or else it would have been necessary for him not to say anything. It was a choice of either the gesture or the dialogue....

NARBONI: Even though at the beginning *Destroy* seemed to be a sort of potential work, that might just as well have been thrown away, or filmed, or played onstage, or read, a potential work that was made real by the use to which it was put, so to speak ...

DURAS: Yes: the use to which it was put by the reader or the spectator. This is the only perspective I can work within now.

NARBONI: So at this point a question arises. *Destroy* is made up structurally of people watching each other at different levels. One of the major axes, for example, runs along like this: someone is watching the tennis court and is watched by someone else, who in turn is observed by a third party, and the narrator, or whatever plays a narrative role, more or less takes up these stories and sees what these watching eyes see ...

DURAS: You see a narrator ...

NARBONI: No, no. There is no narrator, actually ...

DURAS: It's the camera.

NARBONI: There is a sort of perpetual "gliding" that goes beyond a narrator—or the absence of a narrator. What I meant to say is that in a film there is always one last watching eye, which is none other than that of the camera, which overarches all these people who are watching each other. I would like to know, then, in what terms this necessity of having one last seeing eye dominating the rest—that is to say the camera—presented itself as regards the structure of *Destroy*.

DURAS: Does it exist, in your opinion?

NARBONI: Does it exist as a watching eye?

DURAS: Yes: in *Destroy*, in the film.

NARBONI: No, because the expression "watching eye" is not the right one—let's say, then, a last determining factor, a last court of appeal.

DURAS: As if someone wanted to tie the whole thing together?

NARBONI: No, no, not at all like something tying the whole thing together. Not a "gaze," something static, but a watching function, so to speak.

DURAS: Yes, but this watching function can also be called identification with the character. Do you agree with that? With the sacred law that Sartre laid down in an article answering Mauriac, I believe, about twenty years ago, in which he said that one could identify only with one person. To reach the other characters it is necessary, therefore, to do so through the character with which one identifies: if there are A, B, C—A being the spectator and the character with whom one identifies, one must go through him in order to reach B and C.

RIVETTE: Yes. Sartre accused Mauriac of taking himself for God the Father and dominating all the characters.

DURAS: That's right. But this is a law that has applied to spectacle for centuries now. And to novels too. I attempted to break this law; I don't know whether I succeeded. There is no primacy of one character over another in *Destroy*. There is a gliding from one character to another. Why? I think it's because they're all the same. These three characters, I believe, are completely interchangeable. So I went about things in such a way that the camera is never conclusive as regards the way one of them acts or the words that another pronounces, do you see? What either of the men says could also be said by the other. What the other says, the third person, Alissa, might say as well. The men are slightly different from Alissa, it is true, since she doesn't speak of the men, whereas the men speak of her. She never judges. She never goes on to think in generalities. So—wait a minute; I'm lost ...

NARBONI: You've ended up giving us a perfect answer. That is to say that you confronted the risk that the camera might become God as Mauriac conceives Him, so to speak ...

DURAS. This is a nineteenth century prejudice that still holds sway in film-making ...

NARBONI: Exactly. You therefore refused this sort of closure that always makes the camera enclose a space or imprison a character by making it assume multiple roles, in the same way that the characters are interchangeable.

DURAS: Yes, that's it. At any rate, that is what I tried to do.

RIVETTE: This is strikingly evident from the very first shots: shots that I saw in the beginning as representing the watching eye of a character and then in the end, within the very movement of the shot, focusing from the outside on this very character whose eyes the spectator thought he was seeing through.

DURAS: In my script, moreover, there are many directions that point to what you are saying: "So and so is seen watching someone else."

RIVETTE: This was in the book too, but it was indicated by other means—the means of the book.

DURAS: But it is the relation between the people that isn't right, perhaps, in *Destroy*.

RIVETTE: In any case it is a film in which the spectator is obliged to pay close attention (even if he isn't a critic with the typical traits of his profession) to the way in which the camera behaves toward the characters. . . .

DURAS: From the point of view of the camera, I'm not sure quite what I did; you're teaching me things . . . When I planned it, it seemed to me that that was what had to be done, but I did so almost without thinking it out beforehand.

NARBONI: What one finds in it (and what one also finds in a certain number of "modern" films, beginning with *Chronicle of a Love Affair*), is the successful variation of the roles played by the camera, which no longer is content to play a single role as in a certain type of classical tradition, where it dominates the event and where it has an "objective" point of view, but rather has a sort of flexibility in its function, and as a result one never knows whether it is taking up the point of view of a character—for at the very moment that the spectator believes that it is dominating the event, it is taken up by a character, and the point of view thus

97

changes inside a shot or a sequence. This, I believe, is one of the great contributions of modern cinema: a camera that does not have a single fixed role during the entire film, or during an entire sequence, but instead constantly changes.

DURAS: But what would be the equivalent of what you have just mentioned in writing? The role of the author in his book, for example ... No: the role that the author would like the reader to have.

NARBONI: This takes place between the reader and someone who is not the narrator but the speaker. I'm not quite sure, but perhaps an interaction between the two, on the level of the writing itself, in an interaction between the reading of the book and the function of the speaker; I don't use the word narrator, which I find too fixed a term. That, in fact, is why I asked you the question, because it seems to me to answer preoccupations that in the end are all of the same type: what role does the camera have today?—just as one day people began asking: what role does the narrator have? Who in fact speaks in a book? And who sees in a film? ... And I asked you this question so as to find out what equivalence, or what fundamental difference, or what research of the same type you did on the two levels, the film and the book.

DURAS: Well, I tried to write the book *Destroy* ... how can I put it modestly? I don't know. A basic modesty ... I have the feeling that I wrote it in a state of imbecility. And in the dark. And that when I went on to the film, the book seemed clearer to me during rehearsal: its lines of force, its intention, above all politically—but that during shooting I was in the dark once again. I don't know if you can put that in ... And that it was necessary for me to plunge back into the dark so that the camera would have the same sensitivity, if you like, as the pen has when I write. I don't know whether this comes across in the film.

RIVETTE: To try to go on with this line of questioning, there is one passage where the difference between the book and the film is quite striking: the first long dialogue—or perhaps the very first dialogue of all—between Alissa and Elisabeth, which in the book is interrupted by the gaze and the words, the commentary, of Max Thor and of Stein, and which in the film, on the contrary, is continuous, though the spectator may think that this continuous gaze of the camera corresponds to the point of view of the men, or of one of the two men, on the two women.

DURAS: Yes, that posed a problem; that is to say, if the men had been shown watching the women, Alissa would have known that she was being watched. And she would have been a bit more cagey with Elisabeth Alione; knowing that she was being watched, and acting as if she were not being watched. I could not bear the least suggestion of caginess on Alissa's part.

RIVETTE: So it wasn't only so as to avoid parallel montage? Because if I remember rightly, the two women are being watched from quite a distance away in the book: the men are in the hotel, I believe ...

DURAS: They are behind a bay window ... There are voices offscreen during the dialogue between the two women. During the dialogue, there is: "In the bedroom Alissa has no certain age." "It is the void that she is looking at ..." And then I wanted the two women to

99

be alone. It's a long scene. No. It isn't too long? I cut a little bit of it ...

NARBONI: Yes, in the end, if one takes this scene as it is in the book (though one could take some other scene), there is this overlapping that would tend to suggest two solutions in the film: either putting the characters in the field of the camera (which you didn't want to do because Alissa would then have known that she was being watched) or, another possibility, editing this scene so as to show what this passage is intended to evoke, that is to say a sort of parallel montage ...

DURAS: Which, moreover, is already indicated in the typography of the book.

NARBONI: Which is completely effective in the book, and in my opinion would have completely pulverized the scene onscreen. The moment, I think, that the camera had gone from Alissa and Elisabeth speaking to a shot of Stein and Max Thor commenting as they supposedly watch this scene, submitting them ourselves to another point of view, the future point of view of the spectator, I think the principle of the scene would have fallen all to pieces.

DURAS: That's right; that's exactly it. That is to say that this long stretch of time ... Dull. Banal. Dirty and grey . . . would have obviously been broken up. You can imagine how hard I had to fight to keep this scene this long. Many people said to me: "It's impossible; they exchange nothing but banalities." But that's exactly the point ...

RIVETTE: Was it mostly this shot that brought about that sort of reaction?

DURAS: It's the longest sequence.

RIVETTE: I for my part could not have said whether it was the longest or not. Whether it was longer than the card-playing scene, for example. But is it for practical reasons, or for completely different reasons that there are a certain number of shifts of scene from the book to the film? Scenes which, for instance, took place in the book in the main dining room of the hotel take place outside in the film, or vice versa.

DURAS: It was because we had only one room to shoot in, one room and a little adjoining room.

RIVETTE: That is to say that you in fact didn't have a room representing the main dining room of the hotel?

DURAS: Yes, but we finally replaced it with a terrace. We didn't have a hotel building. Someone had lent us the grounds, and an old converted stable ...

RIVETTE: So it's for purely practical reasons that you shifted various scenes.

DURAS: Yes, yes. But there were two possibilities—outside or inside—for all the scenes.

RIVETTE: But did you intentionally change from inside scenes to outside ones, or on the contrary ...

DURAS: This was done deliberately, and what is more, I couldn't do anything else because the weather was bad. I took the scene of Alissa's arrival with her husband out of doors, for example, because I had filmed the preceding scene indoors since the weather was bad ... the scene with the letter.

RIVETTE: The card-playing scene too.

DURAS: Yes, and then too there were some scenes that in any case could only be indoors: there are two of them. Because the dialogue would have got lost outside, it seems to me.

RIVETTE: This is obvious in the case of the second long scene between the two women, which was also indoors in the book, but not in a bedroom, as I remember.

DURAS: It was in Elisabeth Alione's bedroom. No, it was in the dining room. They both act well in this scene.

RIVETTE: And all through the film. The card game is a very extraordinary moment. What Catherine Sellers [the actress] does in this scene is really tightrope-walking. But it is beautiful, because you aren't aware that it's tightrope-walking.

DURAS: It was awesome. Really awesome. Because at the same time there was the way she handles the cards, which changes little by little. She completely forgets everything she knows in a few seconds. But she really did this all by herself: no one can lay down rules for a thing like that. She played cards all by herself at home; she didn't know how to hold a card before the film.

RIVETTE: I had the feeling that the playing of the hands of the three other players around her was very precise, very closely controlled.

DURAS: We focused on their hands: the camera came in close and once their hands were in the film frame they were free, except for Stein, who had to stay in the foreground with his cards. So inevitably he was constantly in front of the camera, rooted to the spot...

RIVETTE: I kept watching the way his hands went in and out all through the shot... not exactly like attacks on her, but almost...

DURAS: We rehearsed the card game for a month. And at the end of the month I realized that it was completely useless to see the others, that their hands alone were enough ...

NARBONI: In the long scene between Alissa and Elisabeth I believe that the mirror enters in quite late in the book, whereas the shot in the film begins a long time before Alissa really enters the space not reflected by the mirror ...

DURAS: Do you know how the scene goes? I've forgotten the book now.

NARBONI: The mirror comes in very late in the scene in the book. They talk at great length and the mirror is mentioned only at the end. It is not present before this mention of it.

DURAS: Is this the scene you like most? In the film ...

RIVETTE: It is not at all a film where one can say: "I prefer such and such a scene." I think that it is really a continuum.

DURAS: I screened it for some Parisians who found the card scene too long.

RIVETTE: Yes, of course, because they really saw it from a ... a Parisian point of view.

DURAS: They find that ... They don't understand. The waltz, for example, of the Italian cities: Naples, Florence ... I didn't follow Stendhal's order, but almost. ... A trip to Italy for a bourgeois is a dance where everything is equivalent to everything else, a trip that is completely cut and dried, that no longer means anything. They don't realize this because they are completely involved in it, do you understand? They are completely caught up in bourgeois life. So they found that it dragged a little, that there were repetitions. I don't care. In any case one cannot make cuts.

RIVETTE: To get back to the question of the role of the camera that we were discussing a while back, there is another moment that struck me, but this time it's a passage that's been cut up, the scene, the next to the last scene, more or less, if one can divide the film into scenes: the dialogue of the five characters around the table, where there is an overall shot that recurs from time to time and punctuates the sequence, and closeups of the five of them; and what especially impressed me was that the closeup of Bernard Alione is from a point of view that seemed to me to be clearly that of Elisabeth, from the very way in which people's gazes are oriented. When the camera looks at him, it is in Elisabeth's place, even during the very long space of time when Elisabeth has left the table ...

DURAS: Yes. That is to say, all the other axes have been abandoned; this gave us some trouble, as a matter of fact, during the montage. We abandoned all the other axes in favor of the one that passes through Elisabeth, and ...

The scene where they eat together caused me so much trouble ... I abandoned one axis completely because from the other side of the window that is in view, from the broad grassy plot, there was a window with bars over it. I could not shift the axis; that is to say, this window with bars over it would have reminded the spectator of a mental institution. I didn't want that. So I had a white curtain hung up. But this white curtain was worse than nothing at all because it gave the impression that there was another room, that Bernard Alione, as seen in the axis of the window, was suddenly *elsewhere*. So removing those two axes resulted in there being only one axis in the end: the one you spoke of.

NARBONI: But this is where the role you would like the spectator or the reader of the film to take begins—to install Elisabeth in the camera's place, and situate even the absence of Elisabeth there, so that the same axis, the same diagonal continues to run toward Bernard. I had exactly the same impression as Jacques—that there was this sort of axis linking Bernard Alione and Elisabeth, that became even more powerful precisely when Elisabeth is supposed to be in the grounds of the hotel . . .

DURAS: It's a sort of line of force, right? since Bernard resorts to Elisabeth in order to know what is happening. He often says: "What is happening?" and looks to his wife to tell him what is going on . . .

RIVETTE: Yes, and at the same time, it's not as if he were judged by her, but still were more than looked at, more than merely observed. It's as if this angle, which has to do with Bernard, made her suddenly see him as if she had never seen him before.

DURAS: That's exactly it. She discovers him.

RIVETTE: She discovers him through the medium of the three others. And the role of the camera emphasizes this fact strongly. . . .

DURAS: She is already inside the dialectic, in a sort of natural dialectic that she has either found anew or discovered . . . But there are two characters who belong entirely to me, and two characters who do not belong to me in the film: I don't know whether this is noticeable. Alissa and Stein are completely familiar to me, whereas Thor and Elisabeth are characters ouside myself.

RIVETTE: Thor is the most opaque character.

DURAS: He's asleep.

RIVETTE: And in the book this is almost more blindingly evident, since the book, more than the film, I find, begins with him, with his point of view, and then the book as it goes along gradually erases him. And it is Stein, who doesn't exactly take his place, but . . .

DURAS: Thor is in a sort of state of catharsis: he is in this state when he meets Stein, and at the end of the book and the end of the film he still is; they are identical. In the end Thor asks Stein only three questions—and it is all over. After that he talks like Stein. As early as the meal they eat together he talks like Stein. They are interchangeable.

RIVETTE: They have exactly the same role as regards Alissa . . .

DURAS: And as regards the Aliones. They are equally indecent. I wanted their indecency to be absolute; I don't know whether I succeeded in showing it to be so. Immodesty and indecency. But natural. . . .

Shall we talk about the ending?

NARBONI: Was the ending of the book as noisy for you as the last shot in the film?

DURAS: No.

NARBONI: Because in the book there is a notation having to do with the importance of the music that is quite brief, whereas in the last shot of the film the sound effects are very important.

106

DURAS: And the poses are different too; in the book Alissa was lying on top of Stein, as if on a plot of ground, a piece of land. She was stretched out on Stein's physical body. This was not possible in the film. A change was necessary because of the image. Because Stein was then completely immobilized by Alissa's body. And the music—in order for the whole thing to take on meaning . . . The music stands for revolution. I had to murder it up to the very end . . . if it had suddenly been very pure and very carefully decanted . . .

RIVETTE: Yes, if there were just the music . . .

DURAS: There would have been nothing left for us to do . . .

RIVETTE: That would have resulted in a purely idealistic aspect, a sort of divine presence descending over the characters.

DURAS: Yes, that's right; and I wanted to avoid that at all costs.

RIVETTE: The way it is, one feels that the music is a struggle . . .

DURAS: I would have liked to distort it even more, but I didn't find any way of doing so. The noise is a piano. It's a Pleyel—what's the name of those big Pleyels—a concert grand? At any rate, one of the big ones. So the scene takes place in a salon in the middle of the hotel grounds, with the windows open and the piano open, and we let the whole weight of the piano lid fall: during the montage the attack of the notes was cut off, and all the harmonics are heard. This is the noise on the sound track. Michael, the sound engineer, and I did it together one evening. But the mixing of the noise on the last reel was rather funny, because the engineer couldn't bring himself to ruin the music. He simply couldn't. I spent twenty minutes urging him to go to it. I gave him superb music and I told him: "Spoil it." He couldn't. And I said to him: "No, go ahead! Go ahead!" Finally he got desperate and did a thorough job of it.—Don't you want to talk about the political side of the film?

RIVETTE: Yes, I think we're going to be obliged to ...

DURAS: Can I read you what I say in the trailer? I'm going to read it. Someone asks me the question: "Where are we?"—"In a hotel, for example."—"Could it be some other place?"—"Yes. It is up to the spectator to choose."—"Don't we ever know what time it is?"—"No, it is either nighttime or daytime."—"What's the weather like?"—"It's a cold summer."—"Is there anything sentimental about it?"—"No."—"Anything intellectual?"—"Perhaps."—"Are there any bit players?" —"They have been eliminated. The word 'hotel' is pronounced, and that ought to be enough to represent a hotel."—"Is it a political film?"—"Yes, very much so."—"Is it a film where politics are never spoken of?" —"That's right. Never."—"I'm completely at sea now ... what do you mean by 'capital destruction'?"—"The destruction of someone as a person."—"As opposed to what?"—"To the unknown. That the communist world of tomorrow will be."—"What else?"—"The destruction of every power ..." I'm perhaps going to change that a little ... "The destruction of all police. Intellectual police. Religious police. Communist police."— "What else?"—"The destruction of memory."—"What

else?"—"The destruction of judgment."—"What else?"
—"I am in favor of . . . closing schools and universities,
of ignorance . . ."—I added the word "obligatory," but
this would amount to decreeing something. Wait a second, I go on: "I'm in favor of closing schools and universities. Of ignorance. Of falling in line with the
humblest coolie and starting over again."—"Of falling
in line with madness?"—"Perhaps. A madman is a person whose essential prejudice has been destroyed: the
limits of the self."—"Are they mad?"—"They may be in
today's outmoded system of classification. Communist
man of the year 2069, who will be the absolute master
of his freedom, of his generosity, would be taken for a
madman today and put behind bars."—"Why a German Jew?"—"Please understand: we are all German
Jews, we are all strangers. This is a slogan from the
May revolution. We are all strangers to your State, to
your society, to your shady deals."—"What is the forest?"—"It is also Freud."—"You say that it is classified
as a historical monument?"—"That is quite correct.
Freud and Marx are already pigeonholed by culture . . ."
—"Well, I'm going to . . . Is it a film that expresses
hope?"—"Yes. Revolutionary hope. But at the level of
the individual, of inner life. Without which . . . look
around you. It is completely useless to make revolutions." That's how it reads. So I'm out gunning for an
entire part, a whole sector of the public . . . Isn't this
perhaps going too far? Don't you think so?

NARBONI: No. But this brings up certain questions.
I am in agreement with the substance of these points,
but . . . do you really think that an inner search, even

one that hopes to bring about a communist society, can suffice to bring about some sort of economic struggle?

DURAS: I am speaking, if you will, of man's passage through a void: the fact is, he forgets everything. So as to be able to start over. I hope that he will thus be reborn, if you will. If this were true, one could return, providing one were exceptionally prudent, to a state of knowingness. Of course. But may it never become a scholastic exercise. An exegesis. Never. I don't know how this will come about. Nor what practical steps to take to bring it about. But I know that, like communism . . . what is communism? I don't know. No one knows. I don't know where this path will lead us. If you like, it's the same way that . . . Knowledge seems to me to be at once suspect and desirable. A certain kind of knowledge. In any case, I am basically against the sort of knowledge that is the province of certain people, the kind of knowledge that is cut and dried—the laws of knowledge.

RIVETTE: But can't criticism of this knowledge that is obviously quite lucid, that is as exacting as possible, also play an active role? Not in the same way as ignorance, of course, and doubtless in a more active way than ignorance . . . I confess that this is an idea that I find at once attractive and terrifying; this is my own personal opinion; there is something that frightens me in the fascination with ignorance: I am afraid, in fact, simply because it is a fascination. I see what this path by way of ignorance may lead to, that is to say destruction as a capital stage, or to adopt a phrase that Jean-

Pierre Faye often quotes: "destruction as a capital moment of a change from one form to another." But at the same time is there not a risk, in fact, of going under within this moment, that is, of going under in such a way as to be entirely swallowed up? Do you really think that wiping the slate clean is the only . . .

DURAS: What other means do you have of catching up with the rest of humanity? What other way do you have of reaching absolute zero? I went to Cuba a while ago. I spoke with students, I talked with people at the university. They said to me: "Should we read Montaigne? And Rabelais? We don't have them here." What would you have answered? Even if I had said no, I still would have been posing as an authority. I said: "I have no opinion." So then. We won't soon see the end of this state of affairs. And it doesn't matter that we won't. It is not because there is no solution that things are in a mess. May was a success. It was a failure that was infinitely more successful than any success at the level of political action, don't you think?

RIVETTE: Absolutely.

NARBONI: But that brings up two questions that I'd like to ask you. The first, which is clearly anecdotal: when you say "Freud and Marx today are classified as historical monuments," do you mean by that that there is a certain fetishism that operates where they're concerned, that completely paralyzes their thought, or that refers to it as if it were dogma . . .

DURAS: What I meant was the Freud used for psychoanalytic ends. Freud can't be read freely. Reading Freud is not within everybody's reach. It ought to be—

especially since Freud is easy to read. But our reading of Freud is already a prey of worldwide interpretation. Yes: when you come down to it, what I said was facile.

NARBONI: I am going to mention a third name that is perhaps also classified as a historical monument.

DURAS: Lenin?

NARBONI: Yes, yes. When the revolution of 1917 took place in Russia, Lenin found himself faced with endeavors that were more or less like a certain endeavor that was undertaken in May, one that I believe you would like to help carry out: namely a sort of *tabula rasa*, a rejection of knowledge that would be the basis for a completely new start along a communist path, and Lenin, at the very height of his practical, political, military, and theoretical activity, always opposed these theories—those of the Proletkult, for example.

2

DURAS: ... it's like doing away with war and talking about it in films: you see what I mean. As long as war films continue to be made, war will be attractive. The films that fight war the hardest are still films . . . in favor of war—except that that's not the word I was looking for.

NARBONI: Yes, it's obvious that pacifist films are war films in the last analysis.

DURAS: That's the way things go all down the line. And so it is with knowledge . . . As far as knowledge is concerned, it should be understood that what I say is absolutely unrealizable. I am smack in the middle of Utopia. I know this. But this isn't important. I can still say it. Just because you don't know where you're going is no excuse for not going on. That doesn't matter at all to me.

RIVETTE: Is it a Utopia to make people angry? Is it a Utopia to mark a limit? To score a point?

DURAS: It's a postulate. Using it as a base, I can write, I can do things . . .

RIVETTE: But is it to score a point?

DURAS: Yes, it may be. In fact, there's absolutely no doubt that it is.

RIVETTE: Because, for example, the phrase that is not in the book and that you've added to the film is precisely: "Books must be thrown away."

DURAS: Yes. Because I throw them away myself, perhaps. It's as simple as that.

RIVETTE: But you didn't put this phrase in the book . . .

DURAS: Because I didn't think about it. Like the phrase on destruction. I didn't put in: "What's at stake here? Your destruction."

RIVETTE: And if you were writing the book now, these phrases would be in the book . . .

DURAS: Yes. But you know . . . young people . . . I know hippies, kids well. My son is a sort of kid too. There is an almost irrepressible repulsion against knowledge and culture. They don't read *anything*. This is something fundamental, something entirely new. Faye is a man who reads. He wants to destroy knowledge, but from *within* knowledge. But I would like to destroy it in order to replace it with a void. The complete absence of man.

RIVETTE: I understand perfectly, but—I won't venture to say that we are scholars like Faye . . .

DURAS: In any case, I've never been a scholar either . . . I've studied mathematics, law, political science— that is to say very . . . vague disciplines. Except for math. And it wasn't because I had a taste for them. Any precise taste. It was more of a mechanism. Do you belong to the Communist Party?

No, no one at the *Cahiers* is a member?

How about you? Are you a member?

NARBONI: No, I'm not, but there are many points,

and one in particular, on which my position would be closer to a . . . a sort of attempt to bring about concrete achievements rather than this recourse to a void. I understand how tempting the notion of "creating a void" may be, however . . .

DURAS: This is what young people are doing, you know. On the international level they are creating a vacuum.

RIVETTE: If it's an active operation, yes, but isn't there the danger, in fact, that this operation of *creating* a void, which is something active, may become a purely passive state?

DURAS: They have to go through a passive stage. That's what I think. They're in this stage now.

RIVETTE: Yes, but going through a passive stage is still an activity. If I may make a play on words . . .

DURAS: Yes, but I don't really agree with you there. Because they don't do *anything*. They excel at not doing anything. Getting to that point is fantastic. Do *you* know how not to do anything at all? I don't. This is what we lack most . . . They create a void, and all this . . . this recourse to drugs, I think is a . . . It's not at all an alibi, it's a means. I'm certain of that. Do you think so too? They're creating a vacuum, but we can't yet see what is going to replace what was destroyed in them—it's much too early for that.

NARBONI: Yes, but if one takes the hippie phenomenon, for example, and if one judges it over a period of years, it's obvious that it soon reached its limit of political apathy, and that a whole sector, in fact, of those . . .

DURAS: In America?

NARBONI: Yes. It's obvious that after a short time,

this sort of parallel world, created by fencing off secondary areas alongside a system that they refused to see (and which also exists, really exists), proved to be perfectly comfortable. And among the hippies, a fraction became politically aware and quit the hippie milieu and became a part of American political activity, joining the SDS and so on.

DURAS: That's true. But they at least had that rest period beforehand.

NARBONI: Yes, but not all of them. Some of them did become politically aware, and others are staying within this sort of emptiness, which may possibly be a first stage, but it risks being nothing but a comfort, it has every possibility of becoming a comfort!

DURAS: But even if they're not politically aware, they nonetheless represent a political force.

RIVETTE: That is to say that by their number, they represent something that is a "gap" in the system, but can this gap suffice to block the system?

DURAS: No, they represent a question, a question that weighs as heavily as a mountain: What now?

RIVETTE: But can this question block the system? On the contrary, isn't this system powerful enough to finally work its way around it, to isolate it, to make it a sort of abscessed pocket?

DURAS: But if this state of affairs gets worse, it will be a terrible thing. If it gets worse, it's the end of the world . . . If all the young people in the world start doing nothing . . . the world is in danger. So much the better. So much the better.

RIVETTE: Yes, but it's like going out on strike. It has to be really a total, absolute, general strike . . .

DURAS: Yes, precisely, precisely. It's like a strike.

RIVETTE: But it's necessary . . .

DURAS: For there to be soviets.

RIVETTE: On the one hand, and on the other hand, the thing makes no sense unless it's really total: unless everything comes to a halt as was almost the case during the three weeks in May . . .

NARBONI: But what the workers who go out on strike do is occupy their factories, and *protect* their means of production. They don't destroy them.

DURAS: Yes; but the workers define the circuit of production. They defend their definition. They are *all* Leninists—naturally.

NARBONI: But I think as a matter of fact that everyone should be; and those who would seem to be the most likely to be because of the time they have available, and because of their intellectual faculties, and so on—are in fact students, who, I think, should . . .

RIVETTE: They should protect their means of production too.

DURAS: That is to say?

RIVETTE: That is to say their capacity . . .

DURAS: What are they? By definition—and here Marcuse is right, though I don't agree with him on all points—by definition they are outside the circuit of production. The hippie is a creature who has absolutely no ties with *anything.* He is not only outside every sort of security, every sort of social welfare, but outside of everything. Of all the means of production, of any sort of definition.

RIVETTE: But the student is someone who is not outside the circuits of production, because finding a place, in one way or another, within the circuit of knowledge is also a form of production after all—one that obviously is not the same as production by workers (we must not make such crude correlations), but there is nonetheless an "instrument" that must perhaps be protected. Not "protected" in the reactionary sense represented by deans of universities, but . . .

NARBONI: Diverted for their own benefit.

RIVETTE: But not destroyed. What I mean is: the reactionary use of this instrument must be destroyed, but not the instrument itself.

DURAS: That would be the ideal. But this is not possible in practice.

NARBONI–RIVETTE: Why isn't it possible?

DURAS: I for my part wanted the action committees to go into the factories and have the workers lecture to us. It would be necessary to completely reverse the roles. I didn't want the workers to be told anything. There is, if you like, something to this business of going into the factories and taking them over that is . . . something like a continuation of Stalinism. Because . . .

NARBONI: Or a continuation of populism . . .

DURAS: It's the most backward sort of workers' movement; it's a fantastic danger. And every neophyte falls into this trap; it can't be avoided.

RIVETTE: It's a form of nineteenth century charity . . .

DURAS: Absolutely . . . paternalism . . .

RIVETTE: There's a worker-priest side to it that is very dangerous . . .

DURAS: The worst possible thing.

NARBONI: It's precisely at this point that I can no

longer follow this sort of negation, this return to zero, because the gravest risk seems to me to be a deviation of a religious type, an almost religious conception of revolution, which to my mind is very dangerous.

DURAS: I don't see the religious side you see. A void is something that you live. There is no religion based on a void. Or, if you will, there is an age-old instinct that impels these young people to go in for almost any sort of mysticism, whether it be Maoism or Hinduism, for the moment, but I think this is an incidental factor. That's all the farther it goes. Or else, you might put it that China is having a great mystico-communist experience; I quite agree. I also believe that they *are* trying to reach the zero-point; but they are taking a very unusual path to get there. For obviously the cult of personality . . . But it is doubtless necessary to go by way of this axis, this pivot-point: Mao is like a sort of geographical point, perhaps, nothing more. As one says "Mao's China" . . . a rallying point . . . Perhaps it's different from what happened in Russia. One hopes so . . .

NARBONI: The idea underlying the principle of *destroy* is that once a type of real communication between people is re-established . . .

DURAS: An almost physical type, if you will . . .

NARBONI: . . . the revolution will follow. I don't believe this. I don't believe that if people managed to talk to each other, to communicate, this would be enough to necessarily bring about revolution. This seems to me to obscure a fundamental problem, one that doesn't stem from individual, intersubjective relations —that of class struggle.

DURAS: You are right. But is it revolution that has

made the revolution? Do you believe in revolutions ordered up from Yalta? And in like manner: is it poetry that made poetry? I don't believe so. I think that all of Europe is a prey to false revolutions. Revolutions against people's will. So then, what *will* make revolution?

NARBONI: To get back to this idea of a void, of clean hands almost—I really think that this is to fall back into a sort of abstract idea of a rejection of every thing that is almost Christian . . .

DURAS: No, it's not a rejection; it's a waiting period. Like someone taking his time. Before committing himself to act. That's the way I see it . . . It is very hard to pass from one state to another. Abruptly. It is even abnormal, unhealthy. If you like, the changeover by the popular democracies from 1940 to 1945 was a brutal one, one not freely consented to and . . . It is necessary to wait . . . You don't do something unless you *undo* what's gone before.

NARBONI: Granted that you *undo* it, but you don't *deny* it by a show of force, by another *diktat* . . .

DURAS: This wasn't a *diktat* . . .

NARBONI: . . . which consists of saying: I place myself on the outside; the inside is gigantic and monumental; I'm not there, so it doesn't exist.

DURAS: You're nonetheless taking the point of view of political ethics when you talk about all this, I think. There's a gap between hope and despair, if you will. Where it's both together. A gap that can't be described yet. I think it escapes description. It is what I call the void, the zero point. Perhaps the word "void" is going too far . . . the zero point. The neutral point. Where

sensitivity regroups, if you will, and rediscovers itself
. . . Anyway: it is said that there are more and more
disturbed people. Madmen: mental institutions every-
where are full of them. This to me is profoundly re-
assuring. It clearly proves that the world is intolerable
and that people feel it to be so. It merely proves that
people's sensitivity is increasing. And intelligence . . .
Do you see? I think that we must turn ourselves around.
We must reason backwards now about many things.
Everybody is neurotic, of course, because everybody is
well aware that the world is intolerable. More and more
so. And a place where we can't even breathe. Do you
agree with this?

NARBONI: Absolutely. These are precisely the conse-
quences of that state of affairs.

DURAS: But it's a hope that I'm expressing. I hope
that there will be more and more madmen: I make this
statement with pleasure, with satisfaction. Personally.
It proves that the solution is near. The premises of a
solution. Because I know that we are very, very far
away. But here we touch on the problem of freedom.
This very moment. We're on the very edge of it.

RIVETTE: What disturbs me is the fact that people
don't want to think about the work that the person
must do, work that your will sets before you at the zero
point. I believe there is no escaping the work one has
to do on oneself, by oneself.

DURAS: But is this work in the strict sense? You
know that work was invented in the nineteenth century . . .

RIVETTE: No, I'm speaking of a kind of work . . .

DURAS: Inside the self?

RIVETTE: Inside and outside: an interaction, in fact, between one's action on what for convenience' sake is called the outside and then the reflux, the return of one's outer action back onto oneself . . .

DURAS: But one can't escape this. And this action is always irreplaceable; it always remains strictly personal. No one can ever put himself in the place . . .

RIVETTE: That is exactly why it seems indispensable to me for this zero point to be lived precisely as work, and not as something to which one would abandon oneself. Because from the moment that one abandons oneself to it, there is the danger of purely and simply remaining there, and getting bogged down . . .

DURAS: Good enough. And after that?

RIVETTE: And after that being duped. Being duped in one way or another.

DURAS: Yes. But I much prefer being duped like that.

RIVETTE: But when I say duped, I don't mean being carted off to an insane asylum, for example; I mean duped because one has got caught up in a myth that is just as alienating as the old myths.

DURAS: Yes, but then one would be responsible for one's own alienation. These young people don't want to do anything. Anything at all. They want to be bums. I have a son who doesn't want to do anything. He says straight out: I don't want to do *anything*. He wrote me one day saying: "Be carefree parents; don't feel responsible for my adolescence any more; I don't want to be a success at anything in my life; that doesn't interest me. I'll never do anything." He went off traveling all through North Africa . . . And he was often hungry; he was very thin when he came back. He took respon-

sibility for the whole thing on his own shoulders. A
sort of exemplary freedom, that I respect. It would be
impossible to force work in an office, or a job as a
messenger boy, as a TV assistant on this boy; I don't
think I have any right to do that.

RIVETTE: Absolutely. And when you say respect, I
understand the word very well; as a matter of fact it is
not anybody's place to impose, and even perhaps to
propose, any sort of solution at all, but the respect that
people have where such things are concerned . . .

DURAS: Do you have children?

RIVETTE: No.

DURAS: Don't get the idea that things were easy for
me before I arrived at the point where I said to my
son: "Do what you want to." I had to do a fantastic
amount of work on myself. Moreover, I believe I
wouldn't have written *Destroy* if I hadn't had this
child. He's wild. He's impossible, but he has found
something . . . something that's outside of all the rules.
A freedom. He enjoys the use of his freedom. He pos-
sesses it. This is extremely rare. And I often observe
hippies: my son goes around with them, there's a whole
group of them . . . What is curious is that when you
go from one to the other, you see hardly any difference
at all in their relations with adults. It is within the
group that they become different, do you see what I
mean? They form a sort of common front against us.
A friendly one. Not a violent one. But they all turn the
same face toward us. When you come right down to it,
you can't get to know them. You're going to think that
it's because I have this son that I defend hippies: that
would be too simple . . . One of his pals slept through
the baccalaureat exam. They found him there asleep.

Not a word. He didn't write a single word. But we've got far away from the film ...

RIVETTE: Not all that far ...

DURAS: Were you perhaps shocked by the violence? By the way Bernard Alione was attacked during the meal together? I cut some of the violence out ...

NARBONI: On the contrary, I found this scene very powerful and very true to life, all the more so in that it was a very difficult scene to do and the character Bernard might have been rejected early on and relegated to a sort of position as an outsider that would have been comfortable for the others, for the spectator, for the film, and for the director too ...

DURAS: He isn't lost, is he?

RIVETTE: Exactly. I was very much afraid, during all the beginning of the scene, that it would become a real ...

DURAS: A trial? That was the danger ...

RIVETTE: And to be truthful, I was more than relieved at the precise moment it became clear that he too could be "saved"—that isn't the proper word. ...

DURAS: Changed.

RIVETTE: Yes, that's it.

DURAS: He asks to stay. One day.

RIVETTE: And we realize he can be loved ... too.

DURAS: That's right.

RIVETTE: And that moment is the point of greatest intensity in your film, and after it ...

DURAS: To me it's the moment ... yes, there's no doubt that it's the one that's most important. "We could love you too." When they tell him that, they are being absolutely sincere. Aggression had to be prevented. They are indiscreet. They are immodest. But they don't attack Bernard Alione. I don't know, though, if that's the way it appears in the film . . . I didn't have them eat, you see. That may interest you. Because Bernard Alione would have been the only one eating. As in the book. He would have been ridiculous simply because he was eating, whereas eating is something that everybody does, both people who are asses and people who are not. So I eliminated this false ridiculousness . . .

NARBONI: And Gélin acquitted himself remarkably well in this scene.

DURAS: I replaced certain things. When Stein asks Gélin: "What sort of work do you do?" for example. Before, in the book, he answered: "Canned food." Now he answers: "I'm a real-estate promoter." I thought "canned food" was too easy a way to ridicule him . . . It has something touching about it, and something naive too. . . .

NARBONI: And the sort of haste on the part of Elisabeth, who finally almost goads Bernard into leaving just when he's been asked outright to stay—do you intend this to be interpreted as a still greater distance from people, perhaps, than that of her husband, or a panicked reaction on the part of someone who feels close to . . .

DURAS: This is the last time she panics. After this her panic disappears. The last death-throes, if you like. Before she dies to her former life. When they say to her: "You vomited," it's her life that she's vomited out. She doesn't know this. All she knows is that it was gratifying. Elisabeth expresses herself in this movement. She leaves to protect her "interests," interests that she then vomits up.

NARBONI: In the book there was a sentence about

Elisabeth that I don't remember in the film, a very severe phrase, something like: "She is not capable of loving," or "she will never love . . ."

DURAS: I took it out. The book had: "She could have loved you . . . If she'd been capable of loving." It was too much. It rang false.

NARBONI: And the film thereby emphasizes even more the "final panic" aspect of the scene. The book seems less forgiving at the end.

RIVETTE: All the times she panics . . . It's something I didn't think of at all when I saw the film—I suddenly had the feeling that the whole thing acted like successive emergences, from deeper and deeper levels, of material that Elisabeth has previously repressed, and that the film works somewhat as analysis does. I doubtless felt this very deeply during the film . . .

DURAS: The card scene especially. It's practically an analysis . . .

RIVETTE: The whole thing . . . But once we've said this, we doubtless shouldn't push the point too far, otherwise one would be tempted much too quickly to see Stein as the analyst, for example, whereas in fact, the roles are much more . . .

DURAS: Evenly divided. Shared. During the meal.

RIVETTE: Not only during the meal, but throughout the film: that is why the film cannot be reduced to a linear interpretation that one can immediately grasp: all through the film there is that elusiveness, that famous "gliding" from one role to another, so that it could just as well have been Max Thor as Stein, as Alissa too in a certain way, since all of them are in one way analysts, and also in another way analysands. Except that Elisabeth, perhaps, is purely and simply an analysand.

DURAS: She remains an analysand. Except for one moment in the mirror scene, where the roles slip . . . where the censorship, particularly of the relation between persons, is lifted. The identity of Stein and Thor that I spoke about, which makes them practically interchangeable at the end of the film, shows up at a certain moment during the mirror scene: "How much we look alike" . . . Isn't that right? That is to say, there is a "gliding," as you put it, from Elisabeth to Alissa. For a few seconds they are one and the same. This can be called love. Or the demand that communism makes.

NARBONI: I find the film quite a bit more complex than the book. In the book one has somewhat the impression—which one loses in the film—that Stein is something of a dispenser of wisdom.

DURAS: He says one thing about there being no need to suffer any more that illustrates what you are saying: "It's not worth it to suffer, Alissa, not ever again, not anybody, it's not worth it." This is more or less what Bakunin said: "The people are ready . . . They are beginning to understand that they are in no way obliged to suffer." Blanchot was . . . I don't want to distort his thought. Anyway, he wrote me a very upsetting letter. He hasn't seen the film yet. He said that to him Alissa was the pivot of the book, he saw her as continually seesawing between death and life. He saw her as facing death continually. Always on the point of being struck dead. At each minute of her life . . . People have said: "Stein is Blanchot." For Philippe Boyer, in *Quinzaine*, Stein is the one who "speaks the desire of Thor," and who is going to allow him to go beyond modesty, the rules of the outside world, the world of order. For him Alissa is—I quote: "the one who destroys and who brings on madness in all its power." Many people have said that the characters in *Destroy* are mutants. That Stein especially is a mutant. I more or less agree.

NARBONI: What struck me most was a sort of passage from numbness, in the full sense of the word . . .

DURAS: A hippie numbness, almost . . .

NARBONI: . . . to a waking state.

DURAS: In Stein? Or in everybody?

NARBONI: In all the characters. It is a film on a state of drowsiness, with escapes, with arousals from this state of numbness . . .

DURAS: That pleases me a great deal. I was very frightened while I was writing it. I was fear itself. I can't tell you the state I was in. A genuine fear though. Maybe that's what you were saying when . . . Or else the fear of being overcome by this numbness. I had no idea where it would take me. Or else I was afraid I'd wake up.

NARBONI: The word "destroy" comes much later in the film than in the book: "Destroy, she said." And the film has: "She said: 'destroy.' "

DURAS: Because this caused lots of misunderstandings. Because, when Thor and Alissa said it, when it was said as one person to another, between just the two of them, people thought that it was a reference to an erotic intimacy that did not concern the others. In the film the word is said in public. I take it to be a slogan. Otherwise . . .

DURAS: . . . that's exactly what Lacan says about the word "Stein."

RIVETTE: With its German meaning of "stone" as well . . .

DURAS: Yes. *Lol V. Stein:* paper wings; V., scissors; Stein, stone. Lacan had me meet him one night in a bar at midnight. He frightened me. In a bar in a basement. To talk to me about *Lol V. Stein.* He told me that it was a *clinically perfect* delirium. He began to ask me questions. For two hours. I more or less staggered out of the place.

RIVETTE: But he didn't say anything to you about *Destroy?*

DURAS: No. I don't think he'd read it yet. Perhaps he'll be sorry about the displaced person Lol V. Stein. I don't know. Blanchot talks to me about Alissa in that letter. He sees her "in the first stage of the relationship with death, in the death that she deals, and that she continually meets." He says that we are all going to *wreak* capital destruction. He says *wreak, make* destruction. This *wreak* delights me. Blanchot is someone who fills you with love and joy. I am aware of what he says about Alissa when I see the film. Alissa may

die for approaching Elisabeth Alione . . . Do you find
her disturbing? I personally find her very disturbing . . .
She wants to kill. That young girl from where?—from
Manchester. That little English girl makes me think
of Alissa . . . That little murderess. She is constantly
seesawing between loving and killing. I hope this comes
through in the film?

RIVETTE: And at the same time this is balanced by
her penchant for breaking things, as if she could break
herself . . .

DURAS: Perhaps because I wanted her to be very
physical. The first thing we know about Stein, for example, is the word "Stein," as the word has its effect
on her. She says "Stein" . . . She takes the word inside
her body. And then when she sees Stein, this merely
confirms things. Alissa to me is completely physical . . .
if you like. At a certain moment she talked too much,
and I cut all that out. She talks more in the book than
in the film.

RIVETTE: In the film she acts by coming closer, by
making contacts, even at a distance, by . . .

DURAS: Tropisms . . . Nobody can bear her except
Stein. I think that's what Blanchot means; she is not
made for living and yet she is alive.

RIVETTE: She is discomfort, in the strongest sense . . .

DURAS: Yes. That is to say: she is anxiety itself.
Lived anxiety. Lived innocently and with no recourse
to speech. I can't talk about a character; I tell myself
that the actors are going to read the thing, and say:
see, she prefers Alissa to Stein . . . No, Stein is the
character most like a brother to me.

Would you like us to talk about conditions while shooting? The film was shot in fourteen days, after a month and a half of rehearsals, and it cost $44,000. I don't know whether that will interest your readers.

. . . Just imagine: I have a hundred and thirty-six shots.

RIVETTE: A hundred and thirty-six? I would have said many fewer. I would have said fifty.

DURAS: There were a hundred and thirty-six shots, but a good sixty of them weren't used. The closeups of the meal. But I realized *after* shooting, during the rough cut, that what was interesting was the impact, for instance during the card game, of the other characters' words on Bernard Alione. It wasn't the others saying "we're German Jews," it was Bernard Alione reacting to this. Or rather having it thrown at him. Then we cut down drastically on the number of closeups in general. But in fourteen days . . . Just imagine: we sometimes shot closeups one after the other, without even numbering them—if you can imagine. That could have been dangerous. But it didn't matter. One must let oneself go.

RIVETTE: What do you mean "let oneself go"?

DURAS: Oh, I let myself drift along. Because I had used a certain emptiness in me as a starting point of the book. I can't justify that now. After the fact. There are things that are very obscure. Which aren't clear to me at all, even now. In the film. But which I want to leave like that. It doesn't interest me to clear them up. For example, the direction all through the scene of Alissa arriving. . . .

131

NARBONI: . . . To what extent do you feel more or less tied to adaptations of your own novels? You have worked on several of them.

DURAS: *Destroy* cancels out the rest of them.

NARBONI: Even *La Musica*?

DURAS: This was a deliberate gamble; the conversation itself was the subject of the film. The bet paid off, but . . . Were you afraid when you saw *Destroy*?

RIVETTE: Yes. Fear, as a matter of fact, that the film would stop being uncomfortable.

DURAS: I've been told that it's a frightening film. It frightens me.

RIVETTE: I was afraid that it would be a film that would stop being frightening.

DURAS: But *Destroy* represents a break with everything that I've written for films: the couple . . . It doesn't interest me any more at all now to do what I've already done before. I'd like to make another film on a text that I'm writing. It's called: *Gringo's Someone Who Talks*.

RIVETTE: Would it be written directly for the screen?

DURAS: No. Another one of those famous hybrid texts . . . And it would be a little like *Destroy* as well, that is to say a sort of superexposition of certain things —and the intrusion of the unreal, but not a voluntary one. That is to say that when it happens I leave it in. I don't try to pass it off as realism.

RIVETTE: I wouldn't use the word "unreal."

DURAS: I nonetheless believe that that word isn't far off. But when I say the word "superexposition," does it mean anything to you? And if I use the word "unreality," you don't see. How about if I use the word "surreality"?

RIVETTE: Yes, I'd understand that better, except that "surrealism" has the same connotations.

DURAS: Hyper-reality. Yes. But where are we? This film . . . is not psychological in any way. We're not in the realm of psychology.

RIVETTE: We're, rather, in the realm of the tactile.

DURAS: Yes, that suits me fine . . . That cuts me off from everything else in a strange sort of way. The book too. Except for certain other books, such as *Lol V. Stein*, and *The Vice-Consul*. That still is all right with me. But the others . . . In *Moderato Cantabile* I was still getting in my own way. This was less true afterwards . . . But as for *Destroy*, I was really quite comfortable. Even though I was afraid. And at the same time, completely free. But frightened to death of being free . . .